NO TIME FOR PRAYERS

There was chaos as Germans rushed toward that side of the church and opened fire and the GIs tried to pick themselves up from the floor. Shattered German bodies lay beneath the stained-glass windows, the victims of hand grenades.

Mahoney, on one knee, hid behind a pew and fired his carbine on automatic at the Germans, his head filled with memories of his Catholic childhood in Hell's Kitchen and his days as a choirboy at Saint Paul's. Never had he dreamed that he'd be killing people in a church, but that's what he was doing.

A German raised his head behind a pew, and Mahoney simultaneously fired a burst at him, tearing off the top of the German's head. . . .

Bantam Books by Gordon Davis
Ask your bookseller for the books you have missed

THE LIBERATION OF PARIS
—THE SERGEANT #4

DOOM RIVER—THE SERGEANT #5

SLAUGHTER CITY—THE SERGEANT #6

THE SERGEANT # 6

SLAUGHTER CITY

Gordon Davis

BANTAM BOOKS
TORONTO · NEW YORK · LONDON · SYDNEY

SLAUGHTER CITY: THE SERGEANT #6
A Bantam Book/October 1981

Created by Walter Zacharius

All rights reserved.
Copyright © 1981 by Kensington Publishing Corp.
Cover art copyright © 1981 by Bantam Books, Inc.
This book may not be reproduced in whole or in part, by
mimeograph or any other means, without permission.
For information address: Bantam Books, Inc.

ISBN 0-553-14712-9

Published simultaneously in the United States and Canada

PRINTED IN THE UNITED STATES OF AMERICA

0 9 8 7 6 5 4 3 2 1

THE SERGEANT #6

SLAUGHTER CITY

ONE

The night sky flashed with explosions as German shells rained down on the First Battalion. The GIs huddled in trenches or hid behind trees, exhausted and in disorder because the Germans had just counterattacked and pushed them back across the Moselle River.

M. Sgt. C. J. Mahoney lay sprawled in a trench, blood leaking through the bandage on his left shoulder. He was unconscious, with jaw hanging open and face pale. Private Grossberger, the medic, felt his pulse while Corporal Cranepool looked on anxiously.

"How is he?" asked Cranepool, a lanky young soldier from Iowa.

"He's lost a lot of blood, but he'll be okay," replied Grossberger, whose thick eyeglasses were taped to his face. "I think we should take him back to the dressing station so they can get the bullet out."

"Where's the dressing station?"

"I don't know—back there someplace." Grossberger motioned with his chin toward the rear lines.

"I'll take him back," Cranepool said. "You look after the wounded here."

"Right."

German machine-gun bullets stitched along the top of the trench, and Cranepool and Grossberger ducked. A German artillery shell exploded twenty yards away, making the ground shudder and sending clods of mud flying through the air. Someone shouted for the medic. Grossberger adjusted his haversack full of medicine and bounded out of the trench. He was five foot four and ran quickly as a squirrel across the tumultuous battlefield.

Cranepool looked down at Mahoney. Grossberger had

given Mahoney a shot of morphine a few minutes before, and Mahoney still was out like a light. Mahoney's left sleeve was soaked with blood. The wound wasn't bad, but the bleeding would have to be stopped soon.

Cranepool kneeled in front of Mahoney and pulled Mahoney toward him. He leaned Mahoney over his shoulder and tried to lift him off the ground, but Mahoney weighed 225 pounds, and it wasn't easy.

"What the fuck are you trying to do?" Mahoney asked in a low, slurring voice.

Cranepool let Mahoney drop against the wall of the trench. Mahoney's eyes were half open, and he had a silly grin on his face.

"How you feeling, sarge?" Cranepool asked.

"Not bad at all," Mahoney replied as though he were talking in his sleep. "What the hell's going on?"

"I was gonna carry you back to the dressing station."

"What for?"

"So's a doctor can take that bullet out of your arm."

"Bullet in my arm?" Mahoney asked in a singsong voice. He looked toward his left shoulder and saw the bloody mess. "Oh, yeah, there's a bullet in my arm."

"Do you think you can stand up, sarge?"

"Sure I can stand up."

Mahoney tried to rise but only got a few inches off the ground and then collapsed into the mud again.

"I think I'm gonna stay right here," Mahoney said.

Cranepool looked around and saw Pfc. Ambrose P. Butsko firing his rifle at the German side of the Moselle.

"Hey, Butsko," Cranepool said. "Help me with Sergeant Mahoney. I gotta take him back to the dressing station."

Butsko pulled the M-1 off the parapet and moved in a crouch toward Cranepool and Mahoney. He was a husky young man with a round, meaty face.

"Where's the dressing station?"

"Back there someplace. You grab one arm, and I'll grab the other."

They bent to lift Mahoney up, and Mahoney looked at them dazedly, seeing them glow chartreuse and pink. He felt giddy from the morphine and wanted to sing a song.

Cranepool and Butsko pulled Mahoney out of the trench

and dragged him back from the banks of the Moselle. The air was filled with the crackle of small-arms fire and the thunder of artillery explosions. It still was raining, and all of them were soaked to their skins.

"Goddamn, he's heavy," wheezed Butsko.

"We won't have far to go," Cranepool replied.

Mahoney spat a big gob into the mud and thought of what had happened to the First Battalion during the past twenty-four hours. They'd crossed the Moselle the night before but without artillery support because they'd run out of shells for the big cannons and had taken heavy casualties. They'd managed to push the Germans back, and Charlie Company had moved ahead to take a little town called Villeruffec, but then the Germans counterattacked in force with tank support, and there'd been a massacre. The GIs couldn't do anything except run for their lives, and many had been killed trying to swim back across the river. Their corpses were somewhere in Luxembourg right now and soon would be carried out to sea.

"Those fucking Nazi bastards!" Mahoney muttered.

"Take it easy, sarge," Cranepool said.

Mahoney craned his head around and looked at the German lines. "Those cocksuckers!" He stumbled and nearly fell, but Cranepool and Butsko held him up.

"Calm down," Butsko said.

"Fuck you!" Mahoney replied, still twisting his body and looking back at the German lines. "We'll be back, you son of a bitch kraut bastards!" Mahoney raised a big fist and waved it in the air. "We'll be back!"

TWO

In a forest two miles away, Gen. John "Bayonet" Donovan, the commanding officer of the Thirty-Third Division, known as the Hammerhead Division, stood in his command-post tent and looked at the map that showed the positions of his various units. He had a potbelly, was fifty-five years old, and had earned his nickname when he was a young lieutenant in the First World War, fighting with the Second Division in the Battle of the Argonne Forest.

Captain Snyder, one of Donovan's staff officers, approached the map table. "General Patton wants to speak with you on the phone, sir."

Donovan groaned because he'd known that Patton would call as soon as he found out that one of the Hammerhead battalions had been thrown for a loss. Patton hated to give up ground, and he'd probably be boiling mad.

All the staff officers looked at Donovan as he strode toward the corner where Corporal Stanfield sat in front of the field switchboard. Stanfield held up the phone, and Donovan plucked it out of his hand.

"General Donovan speaking, sir."

"This is General Patton," said the deep, bellowing voice on the other end. "I understand that you just let the Germans kick your ass."

"One of my battalions was pushed back by the Germans, sir, but all my other units made it across the Moselle and have established beachheads."

"What the hell was wrong with that battalion?"

"They took the brunt of a rather fierce counterattack, sir. If we had artillery support, it wouldn't have happened."

"How does that sector look now?"

"If the Germans come across the Moselle, I don't know if we can hold them."

"Then you'd better tell me who you think I should appoint as your successor because you'll be relieved of command if you don't hold them."

Donovan swallowed. "I'll hold them."

"You'd goddamn better hold them or else. You've got some reserves, haven't you?"

"Yes, sir."

"This sounds like a good time to use them, doesn't it?"

"Yes, sir."

"I'd better not find out that Germans are on my side of the Moselle, Donovan."

"Yes, sir."

"That is all. Carry on."

The field hospital was located in a complex of tents surrounded by sandbags and covered with camouflage netting. Cranepool and Butsko dragged Mahoney to the opening of the main tent and went inside. They saw the floor covered with bleeding, mangled men who were moaning and groaning. The ones who were conscious puffed cigarettes and stared with haunted eyes at each other and the khaki canvas. The only light came from kerosene lamps that flickered and made weird shadows on the walls of the tent.

Mahoney took one look at the wounded soldiers and decided the field hospital was not for him. "Lemme out of here!" he said, trying to break loose from Cranepool and Butsko.

"Take it easy, sarge," said Cranepool. "Everything's gonna be okay."

"Lemme out of here!"

A wide-hipped old nurse wearing steel-rimmed glasses and army fatigues stood up and looked at Mahoney. "What's going on over there!"

"Lemme out of here!" Mahoney yelled, trying to drag Cranepool and Butsko out of the tent with him.

Cranepool held Mahoney's arm tightly and grinned nervously at the nurse, who wore captain's bars on her collar. "He's got a bullet in his shoulder, sir."

"Let me take a look at it."

The nurse approached, squinting her eyes. Her brown hair had gray strands, and her nose was like a big button. She examined the bloody bandage and sleeve. "Sit him down right here. We'll get to him in a few minutes."

"Lemme out of here!" Mahoney said. "I'm just fine!"

The nurse looked him in the eye. "You'd better do as you're told, sergeant, unless you want to be a private again."

Mahoney stared at her. It was almost unbelievable to him that a female who looked like his Aunt Minnie could talk to him that way. He opened his mouth to tell her what he thought of her, but the captain's bars on her collar paralyzed his vocal chords.

"I said sit down!" the nurse told him.

"Yes, ma'am," Mahoney replied sheepishly.

Cranepool and Butsko eased him down to the ground.

"You two can return to your unit," the nurse told them. "We'll take care of him from now on."

"Yes, ma'am."

Cranepool and Butsko looked at each other, the nurse, and Mahoney, who was sitting with his legs splayed on the ground. He looked like a little boy who'd been caught with his hand in the cookie jar.

"So long, sarge," Cranepool said.

"Take it easy," Butsko added.

Mahoney grunted. The pain was coming back to his arm, and he felt irritable. Cranepool and Butsko left the tent, and the nurse walked away. Mahoney looked at the wounded GIs, thinking that he'd like to kill every German in the world with his bare hands for what they did last night. He closed his eyes and tried to get some sleep.

Col. Walter J. "Maud" Muller, the G-4 (supply) officer for the Third Army, was sound asleep and snoring loudly in his room at Chalons when the phone on the night table rang. Groaning, the stocky, broad-faced officer reached in the dark for the phone and picked it up. "Yes?" he asked sleepily, blinking his eyes in the darkness.

"This is General Patton," said the voice on the other end.

Colonel Muller sat bolt upright in the bed. "Yes, sir!"

"One of my battalions in the Hammerhead Division has

been thrown back across the Moselle tonight because they didn't have artillery ammunition,'' Patton said. ''I want you to see that they get whatever they need because I want them to go back across that river tomorrow night.''

''But, sir, we have a shortage of artillery ammunition throughout the entire Third Army,'' Colonel Muller protested. ''If we draw from our reserves, we won't have anything left for emergencies.''

''This is an emergency, and you've just received an order, Muller. Any questions?''

''No, sir.''

''Carry on.''

The connection went dead in Muller's ear. He hung up the phone, turned on the light, and got out of bed, stumbling toward the closet to put on his uniform.

THREE

Mahoney opened his eyes and saw a nurse's rear end directly in front of him. She was bending over a soldier in the next cot, and Mahoney wanted to reach out and have a pinch. Only the vision of a firing squad held him back. He looked at his watch and saw that it was ten o'clock in the morning. They'd operated on him sometime during the night, and his shoulder was swathed in bandages, but he still wore the uniform he'd had on when Cranepool and Butsko brought him in.

"Nurse?" Mahoney asked.

The nurse stood up and turned around. She was blonde, in her twenties, and not terribly unattractive. "Well, Sergeant Mahoney, you're up!" she said cheerfully. "What can we do for you?"

"When's chow?"

She looked at her watch. "A couple more hours, but I can have one of the orderlies bring you something before then if you'll just be patient for a few minutes."

"That's okay," Mahoney replied, "I can get the chow myself. Just tell me where the mess hall is."

She shook her head. "Oh, no, Sergeant Mahoney, you can't get out of bed yet. You've just been operated on."

"Well," Mahoney said, "it's not as if I had my head shot off or something like that. It was only a bullet in my shoulder. That's nothing."

"It's enough to get you evacuated to the hospital in Granville."

"It is?"

"That's right. You'll be going back sometime this afternoon. Now you just lie quietly there and I'll see about getting you some chow."

"Yes, ma'am."

The nurse walked out of the tent, and Mahoney tried to assimilate the information the nurse had given him. He wasn't sure he wanted to go back to the hospital in Granville because he'd be at the mercy of all the silly nurses and orderlies. They'd have him supervising details that mopped floors and cleaned latrines. It might be months before he saw his buddies again, and he might be assigned permanently to the rear, along with all the punks, sissies, and PX cowboys. Combat soldiers would have contempt for him. He would lose his manhood.

I've got to get out of here, he thought, sitting up in bed. He looked at his shoulder and saw the big bandage. They'd cut his sleeve away so they could operate, and he noticed tiny needle marks on his arm. His shoulder throbbed faintly, and he felt peculiar due to the drugs with which they'd injected him. *I wonder if I can stand up.*

He swung his feet around to the floor and looked at the other soldiers lying in their cots. Some were out cold; a few smoked cigarettes and looked at him. They all lay on plain canvas cots, wearing whatever they'd had on when they were brought in, and had been given only pillows and one wool blanket apiece.

"Going someplace, sarge?" asked one of the soldiers.

"You're fucking right," Mahoney replied.

He stood up slowly, and the room spun around him. Taking a few deep breaths, he wondered if he'd have the strength to make it out of there, but then he thought of rear-echelon chickenshit and decided to at least make the effort to get back to Charlie Company.

He took a step, and it wasn't so bad. The room spun less quickly, and he wasn't as weak as he thought he might be. Once these damn drugs wear off, I'll be all right, he thought.

An orderly entered the tent, carrying a tray of food. "Where in the world do you think you're going?" he asked Mahoney.

"I gotta take a piss," Mahoney replied.

"I'll get you a bedpan."

"I don't need no fucking bedpan," Mahoney said. "I can make it to the latrine by myself. Where is it?"

The orderly pointed. "That way, but it's raining out, and you don't even have a helmet on."

"How much you want for your helmet?"

"My helmet?" the orderly asked, surprised.

"Yeah."

"I'm not going to sell you my helmet! What do you think I am?"

"Ten bucks."

The orderly looked around and lowered his head. "You'd pay me ten bucks for my helmet?"

"That's right, and you can get another one without any trouble because there are probably helmets lying all over the place around here."

The orderly took his helmet off, and he had bright-red hair. "If you're crazy enough to pay ten bucks for my helmet, I'm crazy enough to sell it to you."

Mahoney reached into his pocket, took out the roll of bills he'd won in a crap game at Villeruffec, and handed over the ten dollars. The orderly gave him the helmet, which had a white cross painted on the side.

"What about your chow?" the orderly asked.

"Put it on my cot," Mahoney replied. "I'll be right back."

The orderly grinned. "I don't think you're coming back, sarge."

"Sure I am, kiddo. You can trust me."

Mahoney slipped out of the tent and into the rain. He looked around at the complex of hospital tents, the wounded soldiers being unloaded from meat wagons, and several jeeps parked underneath a tree. The rain pinged on his helmet and soaked into the bandage on his arm. He felt a little lightheaded but otherwise almost normal as he moved stealthily toward one of the jeeps.

Charlie Company still was holding fast on the west side of the Moselle. The Germans hadn't tried to cross the river during the night and now, almost at noon, appeared content to fortify their positions on their side of the river. The GIs sat in their trenches, smoking cigarettes and eating C rations. All were filled with hatred and fury for the Germans because the company had lost half its men during the night and every survivor had a friend who never made it to the safe side of the river.

Master Sergeant Tweed, the first sergeant of Charlie Company, sat inside a bunker with Private, First Class Drago, the company clerk. Drago sat in front of his portable typewriter and still was trying to get out the morning report, although it had been due at battalion headquarters several hours before. But so many men had been killed, wounded, and missing in action and so many could not be accounted for that he hadn't been able to put together a report that would be acceptable at battalion.

The door to the bunker opened, and Captain Anderson, the commanding officer of Charlie Company, entered. He was twenty-one years old and was returning from a meeting at battalion headquarters.

"Round up all the platoon leaders and have them report to me," Captain Anderson said to Sergeant Tweed.

"Yes, sir."

Anderson entered his tiny office, closed the door, and sat behind the little wooden table that served as his desk. He took out a cigarette, lit it, and inhaled, feeling exhausted to the marrow of his bones. He blew the smoke out of his mouth and wished he could get some sleep, but there was work to do. He'd been up all last night, and it looked as though he'd be up all of tonight, too. He didn't know how he could keep going, but he'd have to somehow.

Puffing the cigarette, he thought about last night, and tried to evaluate his performance as a company commander. It had been the first time he'd ever been in combat, and he'd made a lot of mistakes. He thought he should have pulled out of Villeruffec long before he did despite the orders that told him to hold out as long as he could. He'd known for several hours that a dangerous situation was developing there, and he should have ignored the orders. It was becoming clear to him that one of his biggest problems as a company commander was determining the right course of action between common sense and orders. You can't disobey orders, but sometimes you have to. There was a knock on his door.

"Come in."

The door opened, and Corporal Cranepool entered. Cranepool advanced to the desk, saluted, and reported.

"At ease, Cranepool."

"Yes, sir."

"We'll wait for the others to arrive, and then we'll begin."

"Yes, sir."

"Cigarette?"

"I'll have one of my own, sir."

Cranepool took out a cigarette and lit it up as Anderson watched him. He and Cranepool were the same age, but he was the company commander, and Cranepool was only a corporal, although Cranepool had been fighting since the landings in Sicily over a year ago. Anderson had exchanged a few words with Cranepool since taking command of Charlie Company and seemed to have nothing in common with him at all. Anderson was a college graduate and the son of a lawyer, whereas Cranepool was basically a farm boy who, according to the scuttlebutt, could get a little kill crazy in the heat of battle. They were the same age chronologically, but Anderson felt twenty years older than Cranepool. Now, after the bloody events of last night, Anderson even felt older than his father.

The other platoon leaders arrived one by one in Anderson's office, and each of them was a sergeant. All of Anderson's junior officers, and many of his NCOs, too, had been killed during the night. Colonel Sloan at battalion said they'd get replacements during the next few days. Anderson didn't see how he could continue with no officers and only half a company.

He stood behind the desk. "All right, let's get started," he said. "I've just returned from a meeting with Colonel Sloan at battalion, and he told me that we're going across the river again tonight at midnight."

The men groaned. Anderson held up his hand.

"It won't be like last night," he explained, "because tonight we'll have all the artillery preparation and support that we'll need. We shouldn't have any trouble at all."

Buck Sergeant Grissom from the third platoon raised his hand. "If we can have all the artillery we need tonight, how come we couldn't have it last night?"

"Don't ask me," Anderson said.

Everyone was silent because they thought a lot of their buddies still would be alive if they'd had the artillery last night.

Sergeant Rademacher of the weapons platoon scowled. "This stupid fucking war," he said.

"Knock it off," Anderson told him.

The door opened and Private, First Class Drago poked his head inside. "Sir, Sergeant Mahoney just showed up, and I was wondering if I should send him into the meeting."

Cranepool twisted his head around and looked at Drago. *Mahoney was back already?*

"Send him in," Anderson said.

"Yes, sir."

The door opened wide, and Mahoney walked unsteadily into the room. He still wore the helmet with the white cross on the side, and he carried an open C ration can in his left hand and a fork in his right. His bandage was visible, and it was soaked thoroughly, but no blood was on it. He hadn't shaved for four days and looked filthy as a sewer rat.

"Master Sergeant Mahoney reporting, sir," he said, saluting with the hand that held the fork.

Anderson returned the salute, wondering whether to reprimand Mahoney for saluting with the fork in his hand. He decided not to because if it hadn't been for Mahoney, Charlie Company would have lost more men than it did last night; on the other hand, Mahoney should know better than to salute with a fork in his hand.

"I thought you were at the dressing station," Anderson said to Mahoney.

"I was," Mahoney replied, "but I came back, sir."

Anderson looked at the bandage on Mahoney's shoulder. "How do you feel?"

"Fair to middling."

"I'm surprised they let you out of the hospital."

Mahoney shuffled his feet around. "Well, sir, they didn't exactly let me out."

"You're not AWOL from the hospital, are you?"

Mahoney winked. "Ain't I?"

"Good grief," Anderson said, covering his face with his hand.

FOUR

Adolf Hitler stood in front of the red-marble map table in his headquarters in Rastenburg. It was a cold, gloomy fall day, and the heating system was set too high, making the room uncomfortably warm, but army engineers were working on it, and there was every reason to believe that the system would be fixed before the day was ended.

Hitler's left arm still was useless due to wounds he'd sustained during the attempt on his life of July 20. He suffered blinding headaches, stomach cramps, and insomnia, and even now, as he tried to read the documents in his right hand, the print blurred, and he had difficulty deciphering the figures. His little dog, Blondi, paced the floor underneath the map table as if he, too, knew that the Reich was in dire straits.

Hitler squinted through his spectacles as he looked through the documents. They were estimates of troop and equipment availabilities for his big Ardennes offensive, which he was planning to unleash against the Allies in December. He was confident that this offensive not only would stop the Allied armies but also defeat them decisively and in one bold stroke change the course of the war and the direction of history.

Hitler looked nervously at the map. He knew that his Ardennes offensive would never be launched if his armies couldn't stall or at least stop the British and Americans right now, before they broke through the Siegfried Line and entered Germany itself. Time was of the essence, and he didn't know if fate would give him enough of it.

Looking at the British sector of the line, he noted that his soldiers had, in fact, slowed the British considerably. Field Marshal Montgomery had paid a heavy price for Antwerp, and the Allied ships still couldn't use the harbor because

German soldiers controlled the estuaries leading into it. Farther south, *Armeegruppe Patton* also had been stopped. Hitler considered Patton the best general the Americans had and never thought ragged and worn-out German soldiers could stop him, but stop him they did. Perhaps Patton had been lucky and now his luck was running out, or maybe he wasn't the great general that he'd appeared to be. There was a knock on the door.

"Come in," said Hitler.

Gen. Alfred Jodl, Hitler's chief of staff, entered the room with a big smile on his face. "Heil, Hitler!" he shouted, throwing his hand into the air.

Hitler accepted the salute placidly. "What is it now?"

"Good news, *mein Fuehrer!*" He held out a communiqué from the front.

"What does it say?" Hitler asked eagerly, his spirits brightening.

Jodl didn't have to read the communiqué because he already had its substance memorized. "General Balck reports that he's thrown *Armeegruppe Patton* back across the Moselle River!"

"No!" shouted Hitler happily.

"Yes!" replied Jodl.

Hitler pointed to the map. "Show me!"

"Right here!" Jodl replied, pointing to the section of the Moselle near Pont-à-Mousson.

Hitler smiled for the first time that day. "And where else?"

"Only there, *mein Fuehrer,*" Jodl admitted.

"Only there?"

"Yes."

"That small area right there?"

"Yes, *mein Fuehrer,*" Jodl said weakly.

Hitler's smile vanished. "General Patton commands an entire army group. If we've thrown them back across the Moselle, they have been thrown back on a much broader front."

"Actually," Jodl admitted, "only part of *Armeegruppe Patton* was thrown back."

"How big a part?"

"Around a division," Jodl said, not knowing that only a

battalion had been defeated, but every reporting officer had exaggerated a little, and in due course the battalion had grown to a division.

"That means that a substantial part of *Armeegruppe Patton* still is on the east side of the Moselle?"

"Yes, *mein Fuehrer.*"

"Hmmm," said Hitler, resting his chin in his hand. "It's not much of a victory, but it's better than nothing."

"Most assuredly," Jodl agreed.

"It could mean a major change in the fortunes of this war."

"It certainly could."

"Who is responsible for defeating this division from *Armeegruppe Patton?*"

Jodl held up the communiqué and located the name. "General Hans Dietrich Kretchmer, the commanding officer of the 217th Panzergrenadier Division."

"Get him on the phone for me right now."

"Yes, *mein Fuehrer.*"

The former artillery officer walked in long, firm strides to the desk and initiated the series of telephone communications that would bring General Kretchmer's voice to Rastenburg. Hitler crossed his arms and looked down at the map. He believed in the significance of omens and portents and wondered if this small victory was the harbinger of great triumphs to come. It surely indicated that even Patton's soldiers could be defeated, and that fact alone could bolster the morale of German troops in the west as surely as it bolstered his own morale.

If only all my units would fight like the 217th Panzergrenadiers, Hitler thought, *then we could stop the British and Americans and set them up for the great Ardennes offensive that will crush them utterly and forever.*

General Jodl hung up the telephone. "Kretchmer is in the field inspecting his troops," he said. "I have left word that he call you immediately upon his return."

"Excellent," said Adolf Hitler.

Gen. Hans Dietrich Kretchmer stood on a hill overlooking the Moselle River and gazed through his binoculars at the American positions on the other side. He wished he had the troops and equipment to cross the river and attack the Americans again, but the German army was only now beginning to put together the semblance of a solid front in the west after a series of catastrophes that commenced with the Allied landings on the sixth of June. Yet he'd managed, with cooks, clerks, and supply personnel, to hurl back an attack from *Armeegruppe Patton* and was intensely proud of himself. The Americans weren't so great, after all. They could be defeated like any other soldiers.

The forests and roads through which he'd passed to reach this hill had been cluttered with heaps of dead American soldiers torn apart by the ferocity of the battle. The Americans hadn't even tried to defend themselves with artillery and armor. What terrible incompetence. Kretchmer realized that the Americans had only been lucky until now. They'd managed to catch the Wehrmacht by surprise on the beaches of Normandy, but now, if the Wehrmacht could offer stiff resistance, the American army would fall apart. It was simple once you grasped the essentials of a problem.

He heard the screech of tires behind him. Turning, he saw Capt. Fritz Nagle jump out of a *Kübelwagen* and run toward him, throwing the Hitler salute.

"What it is?" Kretchmer asked pleasantly, for he was in a magnificent mood.

"My general!" Nagle exclaimed. "The *Fuehrer* has called your headquarters and requested that you call him back when you return from your inspection of the front!"

Kretchmer's jaw dropped opened, and the monocle popped out of his eye. "The *Fuehrer*, you say?"

"Yes, my general."

"Calling me?"

"Yes, my general."

Kretchmer threw forward his left foot and moved swiftly toward the *Kübelwagen*, with Nagle following close at his heels.

Mahoney sat in a muddy trench, protected from the rain by a tent half. He as smoking a cigar that he'd bummed off the mess sergeant, and next to him was his empty mess kit, licked clean. His belly was full, his shoulder didn't hurt too much, and the only thing missing was a good stiff shot of cognac, but you can't have everything.

He was looking forward to the assault across the Moselle at midnight. Although he wasn't a particularly gung-ho soldier, he wanted to pay the krauts back for what they'd done to Charlie Company last night. They'd killed a lot of good men, and they'd even shot him in the arm. Mahoney was determined to really kick ass when he got on the other side of the Moselle. Shoot first and ask questions afterward. Fuck the Geneva Convention.

"Sergeant Mahoney?" called a voice from above.

"Yo," Mahoney replied.

Private, First Class Drago slid into the trench, accompanied by a soldier Mahoney had never seen before.

"How ya doing, sarge?" asked Drago.

"What's it to you?"

Drago pointed to the other soldier. "This here's a new replacement. Captain Anderson told me to bring him to you."

Mahoney leaned forward and looked at the new replacement, who had the sorrowful, thick-lipped face of a camel. "Just one relacement?" Mahoney asked.

"Yep."

"What kind of shit is this?" Mahoney asked. "One replacement? I need twenty replacements."

"He's the only one we got."

"Just one replacement for the whole company?"

"Actually, he was supposed to come in with the last batch we got, but he got lost."

Mahoney looked at the replacement. "You got lost?"

The soldier blinked his bulging eyes and grinned crazily. "Uh huh."

"How'd you get lost?"

"I dunno."

"You been lost for a fucking week?"

"Guess so."

Mahoney looked at Drago. "Take him back—I don't want him."

"You gotta have him," Drago replied.

"Why have I got to have him?"

"Becuzz Captain Anderson said so."

"But I don't want anybody who can get lost for a whole fucking week. I got enough assholes in this platoon as it is."

Drago shrugged. "What can I tell you, sarge? He's all yours. See you later."

Drago climbed out of the trench, leaving the new replacement alone with Mahoney, who puffed his cigar and felt himself becoming deeply depressed.

"What did I do to deserve you?" Mahoney asked.

"Do you know who I am?" the man asked.

"Not only don't I know who you are," Mahoney replied, "but I wish you'd go away."

"My mother is Betty Grable," the man said.

Mahoney looked into the big bulging eyes in front of him and saw madness and delusion. *This guy's a fucking psycho case*, Mahoney thought. *This time they've given me a psycho case.*

"You don't look anything like Betty Grable," Mahoney replied.

"My father is Charles MacDonald. You ever heard of him?"

"No."

"He's a famous fighter pilot."

"That your name—MacDonald?"

"No, my name's Riggs." The soldier grinned crazily.

Mahoney closed his eyes and shook his head. *I hope this guy gets shot tonight*, he thought, *because I don't think I can take very much of him.*

"Are you saying a prayer?" the man asked.

"No."

"You look like a holy man."

"I ain't so holy."

"Well, that's the way you look." Riggs started giggling and put his hand over his mouth.

"What're you laughing at?" Mahoney asked.

Riggs took his hand away and became very serious. "There are good devils and bad devils," he said, "and sometimes the good devils can help you out more than Christ."

"Oh," Mahoney said.

"You know, mental patients sometimes are closer to the truth than regular people because we hear voices."

"I see," Mahoney said, puffing his cigar. He realized that the man sitting next to him was a full-blown lunatic who'd somehow got into the army pipeline and wound up in his platoon.

"Where you from, Riggs?"

"Butte, Montana."

"What'd you do there?"

"Worked in the mine."

Mahoney wondered what to do with him. The man was an idiot and would have to be watched all the time. Maybe he'd be killed before long and that would solve the problem.

"You know what a walkie-talkie is?" Mahoney asked.

"Sure," replied Riggs. "You talk into it, and it talks back to you."

"Right. You think you could work one?"

"I could if somebody showed me how. Maybe I could get one of those little devils to show me how."

"Never mind those devils. There aren't any good devils in the army, you understand?"

"I already met some in the army," Riggs said with his silly grin.

Mahoney put his hand on Riggs's shoulder. "Look at me."

Riggs looked at him. Mahoney fixed him with his stare. "I'm going to give you the most important job in the platoon after mine. I'm going to make you my assistant as of now, understand?"

"Your assistant?"

"That's right. Hereafter you will only take orders from me, and you don't listen to any more devils, understand?"

"But them devils are talking to me all the time."

"This is the army, and you have to take orders from me, not any devils. I'm your boss. Get the picture?"

Riggs looked uncertain. "I dunno," he said.

Mahoney yanked his bayonet out of its scabbard and brought its point to Riggs's throat before Riggs could get away. "If you ever disobey an order of mine, I'll kill you, Riggs, and all the devils in the world won't stop me."

Riggs panted like a horse that had just run a mile. Mahoney pressed the blade of the bayonet against Riggs's flesh, and the young maniac nearly fainted.

Mahoney puffed his cigar. "I'm nobody to fuck around

with, Riggs. I'm a mean son of a bitch, and you don't want to get on the wrong side of me. Get it?"

"Yes, sir," Riggs managed to say.

"You're going to do whatever I tell you, right?"

"Right."

"Good." Mahoney put his bayonet away and leaned against the back of the trench.

"When are you going to tell me what to do?" Riggs asked.

"Relax," Mahoney said.

"Yes, sir." Riggs closed his eyes, went limp against the side of the trench, and fell asleep.

Mahoney chewed the end of his cigar. *What's this war coming to?* he thought.

Gen. Hans Dietrich Kretchmer stood at attention next to his desk and held the telephone to his ear.

"General Kretchmer?" said the deep, hypnotic voice on the other end.

"Yes, *mein Fuehrer!*"

"I want to personally congratulate you for your brilliant counterattack last night."

"Thank you, *mein Fuehrer.*"

"You have written a brilliant chapter in the annals of German arms."

"Thank you, *mein Fuehrer!*"

"You have demonstrated that the Americans can be stopped and beaten. I shall keep close track of your career from now on, General Kretchmer. I am confident that you will continue to smash the Americans and win brilliant victories. That is all. *Sieg Heil!*"

"*Sieg Heil!*"

The connection went dead in General Kretchmer's ear. He hung up the phone, feeling as though light was radiating from his body. His staff officers looked at him in awe. Capt. Fritz Nagle was thrilled to think that his *Fuehrer*'s voice had just entered the command-post tent.

"Gentlemen," said General Kretchmer, his voice taking on a new tone of confidence, "the *Fuehrer* congratulated us for our great victory last night. However, we cannot rest on our laurels. We can expect the Americans to attack again, sooner or later. When they do, we must be ready for them and hurl them back once more. I know that every one of you will do your best to accomplish this goal. That is all. Heil Hitler!''

The officers shot their arms into the air. ''Heil Hitler!''

FIVE

It was night, and the swollen Moselle River roared through hills and forests. Rain fell in torrents, and visibility was nil. At ten o'clock, Mahoney sat in his trench, having had another good meal and feeling almost normal except for a dull ache in his shoulder. Private Grossberger had examined the wound and said it was healing well. He'd take out the stitches in a few days, and then Mahoney would be as good as new.

Next to Mahoney sat Private Riggs chewing a wad of gum. Mahoney had sent Riggs on a few errands during the afternoon and evening, and Riggs had followed his instructions to the letter, seemingly happy to have the opportunity to be useful. He giggled like a madman from time to time, but Mahoney was getting used to that. The main thing is that he did what he was told.

Occasionally, an artillery shell would fall somewhere, and the random crackle of small-arms fire could be heard. Machine guns opened fire from time to time and then went silent. It was an uneventful night at the front, so far. Mahoney looked at his watch, and it was a few minutes before ten o'clock. The artillery bombardment was supposed to begin at eleven-thirty, and they'd cross the river at midnight. Mahoney and every other man in the battalion was anxious to get rolling so they could pay the Germans back for what they'd done last night.

Mahoney heard the sound of footsteps and looked up as Private Pulaski of the third squad lowered himself into the trench. He held a rag to his mouth, which appeared to be bleeding.

"What's your problem?" Mahoney asked grouchily.

"Request permission to speak with Captain Anderson, sarge."

"What the fuck for?"

"Pfc. Butsko punched me, and that's against military rules."

Mahoney frowned as he looked at Pulaski. He hated men who whined and complained. Butsko was a wise guy and a bully—there was no question about that—but he was a good, tough soldier, and that's why Mahoney made him squad leader of the third squad when Sergeant Cooley was shot last night.

"What'd you do?" Mahoney asked.

"What do you mean, what did I do?" Pulaski replied. "The problem is what Pfc. Butsko did."

"I asked you what you did, and I'm not gonna ask you again."

"Pfc. Butsko punched me because he said my trench wasn't deep enough."

Mahoney shrugged. "Maybe you should've dug it deeper."

"Whether I did or not, Pfc. Butsko had no right to punch me."

"Get back to your squad, you fucking fairy, before I punch you in the mouth."

"Huh?" said Pulaski, holding the rag to his mouth.

"You heard me. Get the fuck out of here."

"But I want to talk to Captain Anderson."

Mahoney bared his teeth. "I said get the fuck out of here!"

"Hup, sarge!"

Pulaski leaped like a rabbit out of the trench and ran back toward the third squad. Mahoney chuckled as he reached toward his shirt pocket and took out his pack of Old Gold cigarettes. A cigarette lighter flicked into fire next to his face, and he turned to see Private Riggs grinning and holding out his Zippo. Mahoney put the cigarette into his mouth and sucked the flame into the end of his cigarette.

"Thanks for the light," Mahoney said.

"You're welcome," replied Riggs, happy once again for the chance to be of use to his platoon sergeant.

"You know, Riggs, I think you're going to get along just fine in this platoon."

"I think so, too, sir."

"Call me *sergeant*, not *sir*. I ain't no fucking officer."

"Yes, sir."

"Riggs!"

"I mean yes, sergeant."

Mahoney heard the sound of running feet, and this time Drago slid into the trench.

"Hiya, sarge," Drago said.

"What's on your mind, scumbag?"

"Captain Anderson wants you to bring your platoon back to the command post to pick up ammo for the attack."

"Will do."

Drago scrambled up the side of the trench and ran off with his head tucked low between his shoulders. Mahoney turned to Riggs. "Tell all the squad leaders to bring their people here on the double."

"Yes, sir—I mean sergeant."

Riggs climbed out of the trench and ran with big loping strides toward the first squad. Mahoney puffed his cigarette, glad the attack was finally getting underway.

The jeep screeched to a halt in front of the Charlie Company command-post bunker, and General Patton stepped down from the front seat. Wearing riding jodhpurs and his pearl-handled revolver, his helmet low over his eyes, he marched toward the bunker and threw open the door.

Sergeant Tweed was the only person sitting in the outer office, and when he saw Patton, his eyes almost bulged out of their sockets. "Ten-hut!" he screamed, jumping to his feet.

Patton saluted him vaguely and charged toward the next door, opening it and entering the office of Captain Anderson, who was wondering why Tweed had shouted *attention*. Now he knew and shot like a rocket out of his chair, saluting smartly on the way up.

"At ease, captain," Patton said.

Captain Anderson relaxed but did not sit down. His heart beat wildly, the last person he expected to see in his office was General Patton.

"I just came down here to make sure this battalion is ready to kill Germans," Patton said. "Are you ready to kill Germans?"

"Yes, sir!" said Anderson.

"Last night, this battalion got thrown for a loss," Patton said. "I hate to see things like that happen, but I guess I have to make allowances. You didn't have artillery support, and I want to believe that's why you were thrown back. But you're going to have all the artillery you need tonight. Tonight you won't have any excuses. Tonight I want you to go across that river and stomp those goddamn Germans. And I want you to keep going until you run out of ammo or shoe leather, whichever comes first. Do I make myself clear?''

''Yes, sir.''

''If this company fails to do its job, I'm going to hold you personally responsible. I'll tear those bars off your collar with my own two hands, understand?''

''Yes, sir.''

Patton winked. ''Good. Round up your company. I want to let them know how I feel about this little matter.''

''Yes, sir.''

Fifteen minutes later, the survivors of Charlie Company were gathered in a circle around General Patton. Rain poured on them, and they carried their rifles at sling arms with the barrels pointed down as they gazed with fascination at the most famous fighting general in the American army.

Patton strolled around the center of the circle, looking the men over and slapping his riding crop against his leg. Despite the darkness, they could see the glitter of his eyes and determined set of his jaw. The rain soaked into his uniform the way it soaked into theirs, and it made them feel good to think that he had taken the trouble to come to the front to visit them.

''Now listen here, men,'' Patton growled, ''I know what you went through last night. A lot of your buddies were killed, and all of you nearly got killed yourselves. Now we all know that it's no fun to lose a battle because Americans aren't losers. By nature, we are winners. Given half a chance, we will win any battle in which we are placed. That's because we're tough and strong and because we love to fight. Yes, by God, we love to fight.'' Patton made a fist and held it up in the air. ''We love to beat the shit out of our enemies and step on his face afterwards. We love to rip open his belly and tear his guts out. We pray for the chance to kick him in the balls and split his head open. Is there any man out here who doesn't feel that way?''

Nobody said a word, just as Patton knew they wouldn't.

"Good," Patton said. "I knew there weren't any cowards or queers in this company. I knew because you're all good, red-blooded Americans. I know you're just itching to get across that river over there and lay your hands on those Germans. By God, I feel sorry for those Germans when I just think about it. I really do because I can imagine what you're going to do to them." Patton pointed to the Moselle River. "You're going to make that river over there run red with their blood for what they did to you last night. There'll be so many dead Germans over there you won't be able to put your foot down without stepping on one of their noses. I feel bad that I have to hold you back until midnight because I know you want to go over there right now. But you have to wait just a little while longer, and I want you to use that extra time to clean your weapons and cover them with a light film of oil so they won't get rusty. If you have some extra time after that, you can sharpen your bayonets so they'll cut deeper into those hun bastards over there. You might want to make sure your canteens are filled with water because you're gonna get thirsty while you're killing all those bastards. And as we all know, tonight is going to be much different from last night because tonight you'll have plenty of artillery preparation and support. By the time you get across that river, those goddamn kraut-eating bastards won't know where the hell they are. Their eardrums will be bleeding, and their brains will be upside-down in their heads. The poor bastards will probably try to run away from you, but I want you to go right after them and kill them like the dogs that they are. And I don't want you to shoot over their heads or at their legs. I want you to aim directly for the center of their backs and bring them down. We're not going to play with them after what they did to us last night. And they probably know it. I'll bet they're shitting their pants over there right now because they know they've made us mad, and a mad American soldier is a fearsome thing."

Patton placed his hands on his hips and walked around in slow, measured steps, looking into the eyes of the men around him. When he came abreast of Mahoney, their eyes locked together, and Mahoney felt two spikes shooting into his brain.

"All right," Patton said in a low, murderous growl, "you all know what you've got to do. Go to it, and God be with you."

Patton strode toward his jeep, and the soldiers in front of him parted to make way.

"Ten-hut!" shouted Captain Anderson.

The men snapped to. Corporal Dowd, Patton's driver, started up the jeep. Patton climbed in beside him, and Dowd shifted into gear. The jeep rocked from side to side as it rolled over the uneven ground, moving toward the road that would bring Patton to Dog Company, where he'd give his next pep talk.

SIX

The artillery barrage began on time at eleven-thirty that night. The big guns thundered in the distance, and the men of Charlie Company heard the first shells whoosh over their heads. The shells exploded in the woods and hills on the other side of the Moselle, blowing trees and boulders into the air. The first barrage wasn't very elaborate and just served as a guide to the artillerymen, who could see where they were landing and make appropriate adjustments. Then, when they had the target area boxed in, they commenced bombarding the Germans in earnest.

The night roared with the constant sound of multiple explosions, and the men of Charlie Company could feel the ground tremble underneath them. They had to cover their ears with their hands, although the shells were exploding several hundred yards away, and they were glad that such a bombardment wasn't falling on them.

Mahoney sat in his trench, puffing a cigarette. His new carbine was beside him, and bandoliers of ammunition hung from his neck. The supply sergeant had given him a new helmet without a white cross on it, and he'd also given Mahoney a few swallows of Scotch whiskey. They'd all thrown their bed rolls and tent halves into the supply truck because they were going across the river with only light field packs. Hand grenades were stuffed in Mahoney's pockets and hung from his lapels and cartridge belt. He had a few cans of C rations and an extra pack of cigarettes plus four Hershey chocolate bars. He was ready to kick ass.

Next to him sat Private Riggs, serious one moment and cackling the next. He also carried a carbine plus a brand-new walkie-talkie that Mahoney had taught him how to use. He knew he was going into battle for the first time and was a little scared.

Mahoney heard a voice coming through the walkie-talkie. Riggs raised the device to his face and spoke into it. Then he turned to Mahoney. "Time to move out, sergeant."

"It's about fucking time."

Mahoney stood up and burped as rain pinged on his helmet. "All right, first platoon!" he yelled. "Let's move it out!"

The men came out of their holes and made their way around trees and over boulders to the banks of the Moselle. The engineers were already there with their stacks of rectangular boats. Mahoney saw the other Charlie Company platoons moving to the river bank, also, and farther down the line he could see the other companies in the First Battalion moving into position.

The far side of the river flashed with explosions as the GI artillery battalions continued to pour it on. The river was wider tonight, for the heavy rains had made it overflow its banks. Mud was everywhere, but Mahoney's feet already were wet, and it didn't matter anymore. When the first platoon reached the boats, they put on life jackets and Mahoney told them to get down. They all kneeled, waiting for the order to load up and go across.

One of the first shells landed so close to General Kretchmer's bunker that it threw him out of bed.

"*Was ist los!*" he cried, on his hands and knees.

The door to his room burst open, and Captain Nagle ran in, stumbling over General Kretchmer and falling down, also.

"We're under bombardment!" Captain Nagle screamed.

"Calm down, you fool," Kretchmer replied. "Do you think I don't know that?"

Both men got up and brushed themselves off. The ground heaved like the deck of a ship in high seas as artillery shells packed with TNT fell all around them.

"Nagle," said Kretchmer, "go to the conference room and alert all units to prepare for an attack. Have the regiments at our rear move up to the riverbank at once so we can meet the Americans head-on when they come across the river."

"But, sir," protested Nagle, "the bombardment is most intense near the river bank. Shouldn't we hold the bulk of our forces back and send them into battle when the bombardment stops?"

"It may be too late then," Kretchmer replied. "I don't want the Americans to establish a beachhead on our side of the river. Get moving. I'll meet you in the conference room as soon as I get dressed. And order the artillery battalions to open fire immediately. Understand?"

"Yes, my general."

"Hurry!"

Captain Nagle ran out of the room. Kretchmer pulled his pajama top over his head and reached for his tunic, thinking that if he could throw the Americans back again, the *Fuehrer* might take note of it and maybe award him the Knights Cross with diamonds.

Mahoney lay on his stomach in the mud as German shells fell sporadically along the front occupied by the First Battalion. He looked at his watch, and it was a few minutes before midnight. Around him, the men of the first platoon glanced around furtively, hoping they would get moving soon because they were sitting ducks where they were. Corporal Cranepool was perched on one knee, peering through his binoculars at the German side of the river. *If that was me*, Mahoney thought, *I'd get a bullet right between my eyes, but that fucking Cranepool can do anything he wants and never gets a scratch on him. God must be looking out for the little asshole.*

"Let's go!" said one of the engineers, standing beside a stack of boats. "Let's load it up!"

Mahoney looked around and got to his feet. "You heard him!" he bellowed. "Get on the fucking boats and move out!"

General Kretchmer marched into his conference room and saw all his staff officers gathered around the map table, mumbling and pointing at the little pins.

"What's the latest?" Kretchmer demanded as he approached the map table.

Colonel Brunchmuller, his chief of staff, saluted. "The enemy bombardment has put much of our artillery out of action. We can only offer meager retaliation, sir."

"Hmmm," said Kretchmer, wrinkling his brow as he looked at the map. That meant the Americans could assemble and cross the Moselle without much difficulty. He wondered why they hadn't used their artillery last night. *Perhaps they were trying to take me by surprise.* "What about our forward units? What do they have to say?"

"They're receiving fierce shelling. They don't dare show their heads."

Kretchmer's eyes flashed with anger. "They'd better get up and start firing everything they have at the Americans. It's their only chance."

"It's hard to do that with bombs falling all around you."

Kretchmer thought of the Knights Cross with diamonds hanging from his neck. "It's not that hard," he said. "I'll show them." He turned to Nagle. "Have Goerdler bring my *Kübelwagen* around."

"But, sir," said Nagle, "surely you're not going out there."

"I am, and you are, too."

"Me!" shouted Nagle, horrified.

"Yes, you." Kretchmer turned to Brunchmuller. "You take command here until I return. Order all units to move to the river bank and stop the Americans from reaching this side. Any questions?"

"What if the Americans make it across?" Brunchmuller asked.

"They won't make it across. We won't let them. You have your orders. Carry them out."

"Yes, sir."

Kretchmer took one last look at the map, gave the Hitler salute, and marched out of the bunker, determined to stop the Americans even if it cost his life.

The team of engineers pushed the assault boat into the river, and Mahoney was on his way to the German side. He and Riggs were traveling with the first squad, and young Cranepool stood like George Washington in the bow of the boat, looking at the other side through his binoculars.

"Get your fucking head down, you birdbrain!" Mahoney shouted.

Cranepool ducked his head. Private Trask pulled on one of the oars, and Private, First Class Novak pulled the other one. The current was strong and dragged the boat downstream. Mahoney looked to his right and left and saw the other boats from Charlie Company also moving across the river. The far shore was ablaze with fires and artillery explosions, but some Germans fired their weapons, and bullets whistled through the air above and around the boats. An occasional mortar round fell, but it was nothing like two nights ago when Mahoney's boat had been torn apart by machine-gun fire and he had to swim to shore holding his carbine in the air.

American machine guns, set on high ground, raked the German positions, and the shells fell with increased intensity now that the GIs were underway. But the current was much worse tonight, and the soldiers had difficulty controlling the awkward assault craft. Boats crashed into each other, and men fell overboard. Other boats were spun around and around by the current and carried downstream to Luxembourg.

"Keep it steady!" Mahoney shouted to Trask and Novak as Riggs giggled and the bow of the boat drifted dangerously to port. "Straighten this fucking boat out!"

A huge log that had fallen into the river upstream sped beneath the surface like a submarine and struck Mahoney's boat amidships. It crashed through the plywood and nearly took off Novak's leg. The shock of the collision caused Private, First Class Berman to fall into the water, and Mahoney watched horrified as water poured into the boat.

"Fuck!" he cried.

Everybody looked at him as the boat began to sink into the swirling Moselle River. Riggs's teeth chattered with fear, but he remained still because he was more afraid of Mahoney than he was of the river. Mahoney realized there was only one thing to do.

"Over the side!" he yelled. "Let's hit it!"

He jumped up and was the first one to land in the water, which was ice cold and chilled him to the marrow of his bones. Riggs splashed beside him, and the other GIs dropped into the water all around the boat.

Mahoney looked at Riggs and thought him more faithful

than a dog. I wish I had ten more like him. "Forward!" he
shouted. "Hit the fucking beach!"

Mahoney and the men from the first squad held their
weapons in the air as they kicked with their feet and stroked
with one arm toward the shore. Then, suddenly, the American artillery bombardment ceased because some of their boats
had reached the halfway point in the river and presumably
would soon touch shore on the German side.

"Oh-oh," said Mahoney, struggling to make his way
through the water.

Sure enough, the fire from the German side gradually
increased in intensity because the Germans were able to come
up out of their holes and take aim without fear of having their
heads blown off.

Bullets zipped into the water all around the first platoon.
Private Wilkerson screamed and writhed in the water as blood
spurted out of his throat.

Here we go again, Mahoney thought. *Why didn't I stay in
that fucking hospital where I was safe from this shit?*

General Kretchmer's *Kübelwagen* moved quickly over the
forest trails. He held on to the windshield with one hand
while gesticulating wildly with his other at the soldiers he
saw nearby.

"Forward!" he shouted. "Counterattack!"

He saw a group of men cowering behind trees and jumped
out of the *Kübelwagen*, running toward them and waving his
hands. "Follow me!" he yelled. "Push the swine back!"

He pulled his service pistol out of its holster and ran
toward the river bank. "Fire your weapons! Keep firing all
the time!"

Captain Nagle got out of the *Kübelwagen* and ran after his
commanding general. He drew his pistol also and rammed a
round into the chamber, hoping he'd never have to use it
because he'd been a staff officer throughout all of his career
and never had been this close to fighting before. Up ahead,
he watched General Kretchmer rallying the men and exhorting
them to fire at the Americans. *Now that's a real combat
commander,* Nagle thought. *Why can't I be like that?*

He followed General Kretchmer and the men with him

until they debouched from the woods and could see the river and the American boats upon it.

"Don't let them come ashore!" Kretchmer screamed. "Blow them out of the water!"

The General soldiers, half deafened from the artillery bombardment, saw their commanding general and thought that if he could run around like that, they at least could raise their heads and fire their rifles and machine guns. Even Captain Nagle was emboldened by the example set by Kretchmer and fired his pistol at one of the boats.

"Open fire!" Nagle shouted. "Kill them all!"

The German soldiers, their heads aching from the long bombardment, sighted their weapons on the American boats drawing close to the shore. There weren't many Germans left, and those still alive were severely disoriented, but they were determined to follow orders and do their duty.

They'd beaten the Americans before, and they could do it again, they thought.

In the Moselle River the GI boats moved backwards, sideways, and at weird angles as the rowers tried to make it to shore. The soldiers held their heads low in the gunwales now that the German fire had increased in intensity. Every one of the soldiers remembered Patton's speech and knew they didn't dare fail in their mission to occupy the east bank of the river. Some of them fired their rifles at the Germans, but the swift current and bobbing boats interfered with their abilities to aim straight.

Captain Anderson's boat was one of the first to hit shore, and he leaped on to the mud and rocks, firing his carbine from the hip.

"Follow me!" he yelled. "Take the high ground!"

The men in his boat followed him, their rifles and carbines blazing. To their left and right, other boats touched shore and disgorged their occupants, who charged into the midst of the Germans, cutting them down with weapons fire and pushing them back with the fury of their attack.

"Keep moving!" said Captain Anderson. "Let's go!"

Anderson didn't take cover because the German resistance was nothing like what it had been two nights ago when

Charlie Company had been pinned down and nearly slaughtered right on the bank of the river. A German rose in front of him, brandishing his rifle and bayonet, and Anderson shot him in the chest.

"Forward!" Anderson screamed. "Follow me!"

Mahoney's finger scraped the bottom of the shoreline, and he came up out of the water like a huge, angry water buffalo. He shook himself off, raised his carbine high in the air, and ran to the river bank, his big feet plunging in and out of the mud.

"First platoon, where the fuck are you!" he bellowed.

He looked around and saw chaos everywhere. Some GIs already were entering the woods, while others were fighting on the beach. Huge shell craters covered the ground, and dismembered Germans lay everywhere. Mahoney didn't know where his platoon was; in the confusion of the river crossing, it had become mixed up with other units. All he had to command was Cranepool's first squad and his runner, Private Riggs, who ran ashore behind Mahoney and jumped up and down like an excited monkey.

"Up and at 'em!" Mahoney yelled. "Charge!"

Mahoney flicked his carbine to the automatic setting and fired a burst straight ahead. German resistance was light—he could sense that immediately—and it made him mad because he'd come to fight and wreak vengeance on the Germans for what had happened yesterday.

Cranepool and his squad followed Mahoney as he ran toward the woods. Mahoney leaped over shell craters and stomped on the faces of dead Germans. A German came out of a hole, waving his hands in the air and trying to surrender, but Mahoney gave him a carbine burst in the face, and the German sagged back into his hole, blood spouting from the sausage meat that his head had become. Mahoney jumped over him and looked through the rain and darkness for more Germans to kill. He saw flashes of muzzle blasts toward his left and headed in that direction. Bullets whistled past his ears, and he yanked a grenade from his lapel.

"Hit it!" he yelled.

He dove to the ground and hurled the grenade at the

muzzle blasts. The grenade exploded, shaking the ground and filling the night with thunder. Mahoney was on his feet again, charging the carnage. He saw a big hole in the ground and movement within it. Firing his carbine on automatic, the movement became more frantic, like a lot of rats scurrying for shelter, and then his carbine made a big click because the clip was empty.

In the ditch, a German officer, still barely alive, aimed his pistol at Mahoney, who dropped quickly to the ground. The shot rang out; a bullet passed inches above Mahoney's helmet, and the German tried to fire again, but from out of the night came a walkie-talkie flying through the air, and it hit the German in the face. Mahoney leaped forward, grabbed the German officer by the throat, and squeezed with all his strength. The German tried to pull Mahoney's hands away but didn't have the strength. The German went limp. Mahoney let him go and picked up the walkie-talkie. He turned around and saw Riggs standing above him, cackling and jumping up and down.

"Hit him right on the noggin!" Riggs said.

Mahoney realized that the lunatic had probably saved his life. He climbed out of the hole and held the walkie-talkie to his ear; it was still working. He handed it to Riggs.

"Good work, Riggs," he said.

"Hit him right on the noggin!" Riggs screeched excitedly.

Mahoney looked ahead and saw Cranepool leading his platoon forward, shooting and stabbing Germans. To his right, he saw Corporal Mason with the fourth squad moving closer to Cranepool's squad. *My platoon's coming together,* Mahoney thought, feeding a new clip into his carbine. He rammed a round into the chamber and ran forward to join his men. Riggs followed close behind him, transfixed by all the blood and gore around him, thinking that somehow he had descended into the pits of hell.

General Kretchmer saw his men falling back and wondered what he could do to turn around the debacle that was unfolding before his eyes. The Americans outnumbered his forces, who had been nearly wiped out by the bombardment, and the German soldiers left weren't in much condition to fight. Standing near the edge of the woods, he saw some surrendering, holding their hands in the air, but the American soldiers shot them down and kept charging.

Kretchmer felt sick and dizzy and didn't know what to do, although he knew he had to do something quickly. The Americans were charging up the river bank and would envelop him soon. He should get the hell out of there while he had the chance, but he didn't want his men to see him running away, and he realized that he'd never be able to live with himself if he retreated ignominiously from the field of battle. The only thing to do was stand and fight and set an example for the German soldiers of the future.

He checked his pistol and saw that he had several bullets left in the chamber. He tightened the strap of his helmet and stepped forward resolutely to fight his last battle. He heard running footsteps to his right and turned in that direction. It was Captain Nagle, a panic-stricken expression on his face.

"Sir, the battle is lost!" Nagle said, trying to catch his breath. "You must order a retreat!"

"Never," Kretchmer replied. "We counterattack at once!"

"Counterattack!" Nagle said. "With what!"

"With the forces at our command."

"But, sir!"

"I have given you an order, Captain Nagle. Follow me."

Nagle was unable to move. Part of him was a trained, disciplined German officer, and the other part was a human being who wanted to escape certain death.

"Nagle," Kretchmer said above the roar of battle, "we all die eventually, but you have a choice between dying with honor or dying like a coward with a bullet in your back. Think of your mother and father, Nagle. What would they want you to do?"

"They'd want me to come home alive," Nagle replied with a catch in his throat.

Kretchmer gave Nagle a look of utter contempt, then turned and walked swiftly toward the fighting in front of him.

"Hold fast!" he shouted. "Hurl them back!"

Private, First Class Butsko and his third squad had come ashore downriver from Mahoney and were fighting their way

toward the woods, making good progress against scattered
resistance. They fired at everything that moved and took no
prisoners as they jumped over trenches and shell holes,
screaming battle cries and seeking revenge for their buddies
who'd been killed yesterday.

They heard a German mortar round coming in on them and
hit the dirt. It exploded to their front, covering them with
muck and pebbles, but before all the debris hit the ground,
they were on their feet again and charging forward.

Through the smoke, Butsko was surprised to see a German
officer of high rank, to judge from the ribbons and braids on
his uniform. The officer was leading six German soldiers in
what appeared to Butsko as a suicide charge.

"Get those cocksuckers!" Butsko hollered, firing from the
hip as he advanced.

His men shot down two of the Germans, and Private
Braxton was hit with a German bullet in the gut, tripping and
falling, doubled up, into a shell crater. The third squad and
the Germans came together and clashed hand to hand.

Butsko was out in front because he loved violence and
infighting. He pushed his rifle forward and smashed through
the futile parry attempt of a German soldier, sinking his
bayonet into the German's chest. The German howled in pain
and horror as Butsko pulled back on his rifle and yanked the
bayonet out. A geyser of hot blood followed it, and the
German sagged to the ground.

Butsko turned, bashed another German in the head with his
rifle butt, and when the German fell backward, Butsko ran
him through the gut with his bayonet. "That's for Sergeant
Cooley," Butsko growled, pulling the bayonet out. He looked
up and saw the high-ranking German officer in front of him,
pointing his pistol at him. Butsko could see that the officer
was an old man close to sixty, lean as a rail. Butsko wasn't
afraid and didn't even close his eyes. He just gritted his teeth
and waited for the bullet that would blow him to hell.

It never came. The officer pulled his trigger, but his pistol
was empty. As soon as he realized that, he charged Butsko,
shouting something in German, and tried to smash Butsko in
the face with the barrel of his pistol. Butsko leaped to the side
quickly as a cat and whacked the officer in the head with his

rifle butt. There was a loud slamming sound, and the officer went flying through the air, landing on his back inside a ditch.

Butsko charged after him, dropping into the ditch. He saw the old officer sprawled unconscious on the ground, and Butsko raised his rifle and bayonet to harpoon him through the heart.

"Hold it, Butsko!" shouted a voice behind him.

Butsko turned around and saw Captain Anderson standing at the edge of the ditch. Blood dripped from the bayonet on Anderson's carbine, and his left sleeve had been torn off just below the elbow. Anderson jumped into the ditch beside Butsko and looked at the old officer, who was bleeding from the ear and mouth.

"I think that's a general," Anderson said. "We've got to keep him alive because G-2 will want to talk to him." Anderson bent down and felt the officer's pulse. "He's still alive, thank God."

"Can I take his watch, sir, seeing as how I'm the one who got him."

"No, because he's still alive. That would be stealing."

"Who'd know?"

"I'd know, and you'd know. Join your platoon and resume the attack."

"Yes, sir." Butsko bent over and took a good look at the watch; if he ever saw it on Captain Anderson's wrist, he'd have a few things to say, officer or no officer.

Butsko climbed out of the hole and joined his men, who were advancing into the forest.

Hiding behind a bush, Captain Nagle saw what had happened to General Kretchmer and thought he had been killed. Terrified, he turned and ran headlong into the woods, hearing gunfire and explosions all around him.

The woods were wet and smoky, with nearly every tree splintered or knocked down. Dead German soldiers lay everywhere, and in the darkness Nagle kept stepping on them. He veered toward the road on which he and Kretchmer had arrived by jeep, hoping the jeep still was there, but as he drew close, he heard soldiers speaking English and realized that the Americans already had control of the road.

His only chance was to keep going through the woods and

somehow get to safety. He ran as quickly as he could, stumbling over fallen trees and wounded soldiers. Some of the soldiers called out to him for help, but he ignored them and kept going.

His throat was dry, and his heart chugged like an old engine. A buzzing sound was in his ears, and he expected to be shot in the back at any moment. He tore off his helmet and threw it away so that he would have less weight to carry. He also unbuckled his cartridge belt and let it fall to the ground. Dodging a shell hole, he tripped over a twig and fell head first into the body cavity of a German soldier who'd been blown apart by an American artillery shell. Screeching wildly, he scrambled to his feet, trying to wipe the blood off his face. His stomach couldn't stand it anymore and went into convulsions. Finally, drained of energy, he leaned against a tree and closed his eyes. *What did I do to deserve this?* he thought. *Why do there have to be wars?*

He felt a hand on his shoulder. "Are you all right, sir?"

Nagle spun around and found himself looking up at a German sergeant. He didn't know whether he was hallucinating or not because the sergeant appeared calm and in control of himself. "Who are you?" Nagle asked.

"Sergeant Uebelhor, B Regiment, sir. Are you wounded?"

"No," Nagle said.

"Then you'd better come with me, sir. It's not safe out here."

"Yes, of course."

Nagle stood up, looking at the sergeant in the darkness and wondering what the sergeant thought of him, all covered with blood and running away from the enemy. The sergeant took his sleeve and pulled him through the woods. After around twenty yards, Nagle saw a white concrete pillbox looking like a huge egg straight ahead. In a narrow slit on the front of the pillbox was the ugly snout of a machine gun.

The sergeant led Nagle to the rear of the pillbox and knocked on the door. It was opened by a private not more than eighteen years old. Nagle stepped inside the pillbox and saw five haggard German soldiers with their machine gun and numerous crates of ammunition.

"How far away are the Americans?" the sergeant asked Nagle.

"Very close," Nagle replied.

The sergeant looked at the machine gun and smiled grimly. "We'll be ready for them when they come," he said.

Nagle, his face smeared with blood, looked at them in astonishment. "Why don't you get out of here while you have the chance!"

"Because," replied the sergeant, "our last orders were to hold fast and fight to the last man."

"But that's ridiculous," Nagle said. "There are hundreds of Americans heading this way. You won't have a chance."

"Orders are orders," the sergeant told him.

"Not for me," Nagle said. "I'm getting out of here!"

He pushed open the door and ran off into the woods.

The First Battalion charged into the mangled woodland area, killing any Germans who were still alive and hadn't had the sense to flee. They moved forward quickly, hoping to find more Germans to shoot because they still wanted revenge for the humiliating reversals they'd suffered last night. Behind them, on the banks of the Moselle River, army engineers were building a pontoon bridge to replace the one that had been blown away last night. Soon the tanks and trucks would roll across the river and head toward the Saarland.

The squads from Mahoney's platoon managed to find each other and move forward as a unit into the forest. As dawn became a faint glimmer on the horizon behind them, they advanced in a skirmish line, their eyes squinting straight ahead for signs of German resistance.

Suddenly, a machine gun opened fire in front of them, and three GIs were spun around by the bullets smacking into them.

"Hit it!" yelled a chorus of voices.

The soldiers who hadn't been shot didn't wait for the order; they already were on their way to the ground.

"Medic!" called one of the soldiers who'd been hit.

Private Grossberger arose and ran hunched over toward the fallen GIs, but another machine-gun burst sent bullets zipping into the ground near his feet, forcing him to drop down and move the rest of the way on his belly.

"So that's the way they want to play," Mahoney muttered, looking for the location of the machine gun. It started firing

again, and its muzzle blast could be seen through the bushes
and the gray dawn.

"On my signal," Mahoney shouted, "first squad, move
out and second and third squads cover!"

The second and third squads fired at the muzzle blast
they'd seen, and Cranepool jumped up with the first squad,
running madly through the brush and hopping over logs on
their way toward the enemy machine gun. After rushing
fifteen yards, they flopped down and began firing at the
pillbox, which they could see clearly now.

Now the second squad moved forward while the other
squads covered their movements, and finally the third squad
moved up, Mahoney and Riggs traveling with them.

Mahoney looked ahead at the pillbox as his men fired at
the little slit in its front. He'd taken about a hundred
pillboxes in his military career, and it was no sweat if you
had some TNT with which to blow in the back door, but he
didn't have any TNT, so they'd have to take it frontally,
moving forward slowly and then dropping a hand grenade
into the slit or firing a bazooka shell through it.

"Corporal Shackleton!" Mahoney yelled.

"Hup, sarge!"

"Get the fuck over here! Everybody else keep firing,
goddammit!"

The first platoon peppered the pillbox with rifle and BAR
(Browning automatic rifle) fire as Corporal Shackleton, the
new temporary platoon leader of the weapons squad, ran
forward and dove into the mud beside Mahoney.

Mahoney looked at him. "Get your bazooka man up
here."

"My bazooka man's been hit. He's back on the beach."

"Then who's got the fucking bazooka?"

"I don't know. I think it's back on the beach with him."

"What!" screamed Mahoney.

"I said it's back on the beach with him."

Mahoney grabbed Shackleton by the front of his shirt and
glowered at him as German machine-gun bullets whistled
over their heads. "You should've given that bazooka to
somebody else, you fucking shitbird!"

"Jeez, sarge," Shackleton replied, "things were happening so fast down on the beach that I didn't think of that."

"Well, I'm not going to think of you when it comes time to make new sergeants in this platoon. Get the fuck away from me before I kill you."

Riggs cackled nuttily as Shackleton crawled away.

"Shaddup, you fucking moron!" Mahoney snarled at Riggs.

Riggs became serious instantly. Mahoney looked forward at the chattering machine gun inside the pillbox and wondered who to send forward with the hand grenade. He didn't want to send Cranepool because he usually picked him for the dirty jobs and it wasn't fair to expose him to danger all the time. Corporal Mason from the second squad probably would get himself killed, and Butsko from the third squad would be a big, slow-moving target. Shackleton from the weapons squad definitely couldn't handle it. *It'll have to be me*, he thought ruefully. *Oh, shit.*

"Everybody cover me!" he yelled. "I'm going forward!" He turned to Riggs. "You stay put right here. If anything happens to me, notify Captain Anderson."

"Where you going?" Riggs asked.

"To fuck your kid sister. Here, hold my carbine."

"But I ain't got no kid sister," Riggs replied, wrinkling his nose.

"You ain't got no fucking brains, either. Stay put and shut up."

"Hup, sarge."

Mahoney took a hand grenade from his lapel, pinched the ends of the pin together so the pin could be pulled easily when the time came, and dropped the grenade into his shirt pocket. He adjusted his helmet on his head and crawled parallel to his skirmish line, heading toward the right so he could move toward the bunker from the side.

His men fired incessantly at the bunker, and the German machine gun returned their fire, sending a hail of bullets over their heads but not hitting anybody. Mahoney knew it was difficult for the Germans to take aim with all the bullets ricocheting around the slit in the bunker. They must realize that someone was trying to sneak closer and blow them up. He didn't understand why they didn't try to surrender or fly the coop. Maybe they realized they were going to get killed no matter what they did.

He ran parallel to his platoon skirmish line, passed the last man on the end, and continued for twenty yards. Then he dropped to his stomach and crawled toward the bunker from an angle that the machine gun couldn't reach, taking advantage of the cover provided by boulders, shell holes, and fallen trees. Looking at the pillbox, he figured that the machine gun couldn't transverse this far to the side and couldn't shoot him even if the Germans knew he was coming. He continued crawling until he felt certain he could reach the pillbox in one final burst of speed, then took the hand grenade out of his pocket. Examining it to make sure he could pull the pin out quickly, he signaled to his platoon to intensify their fire, then leaped up and ran toward the pillbox, the grenade in his right hand. When he was halfway there, he pulled the pin and prepared to let it fly.

He thought the pillbox was as good as out of action as he drew closer to it, running as quickly as he could. Then, suddenly, he saw two Germans come out of the back of the pillbox! They turned toward him and raised their rifles to shoot him down. Mahoney dodged to the side, pulling the pin out of the hand grenade. He dropped to the ground, letting the lever go as bullets exploded into the mud beside him. The grenade went pop, and its firing mechanism became activated as Mahoney continued rolling through the mud, trying to count. When he reached four, he stopped suddenly and chucked the grenade at the two Germans.

One of them tried to catch it, hoping to throw it back, but that's why Mahoney let the lever go ahead of time. The grenade exploded in the German's hands, blowing away his arms and head. Shrapnel sliced the German next to him apart, and Mahoney yanked another grenade from his lapel, pulled the pin, charged the slit in front of the bunker, and saw the machine gun traversing from side to side, spitting lead at his platoon. Mahoney reached the pillbox, pressed his back against it, let the lever fly off, and started counting again. When he reached four, he leaped into the air and tossed the grenade into the slit, then ran three steps and dove behind a fallen tree.

The machine gun stopped firing, and there were shouts inside the pillbox. Then the grenade exploded, sending billows of smoke out the slit. The first platoon charged, flanking the pillbox so that they could catch anybody coming out the rear door. It opened, and a German sergeant staggered out, his uniform half blown away and blood pouring from wounds on his face and body.

Butsko happened to be standing in front of him, and he brought his rifle to his shoulder, firing pointblank at the German. The bullet hit the German in the chest and sent him flying back into the pillbox. Butsko stepped forward at the head of his squad and cautiously approached the opened door. He looked inside and saw blood and shattered bodies everywhere. One of the bodies moaned softly, and Butsko shot it through the head.

The rest of the platoon crowded around the door and peeked inside. Mahoney pushed soldiers out of his way so he could get a good look, too. The pillbox was out of action for the rest of the war.

"Riggs!" he yelled.

"Hup, sarge."

"Gimme my carbine!"

Riggs made his way through the crowd and handed the weapon over. Mahoney slung it over his shoulder and pushed his helmet to the back of his head.

"Take ten," he said, "while I call the C.O. and find out where the fuck we're supposed to be."

The soldiers sat on the ground and took out their packs of cigarettes while Mahoney took the walkie-talkie from Riggs and spoke the code name for Captain Anderson into the mouthpiece.

SEVEN

General Patton woke up early that morning, and before taking a bath or having breakfast, he called Col. Halley G. Maddox, his G-3 (operations) officer.

"Maddox," he bellowed into the telephone, "how'd my Hammerheads do last night?"

"Pretty good, general. They took back all the ground they lost and then some."

"I knew they could do it," Patton said. "They're a good bunch of boys. They've been on the line for quite a while now, haven't they?"

"Ever since they left Paris, sir."

"I think it's time they had a little rest. Pull them back and give them some R & R. I also want them brought up to full strength again because I've got a big job lined up for them."

"Yes, sir."

Patton hung up the phone, yawned, and walked to the bathroom where he turned the spigots that brought water pouring into his bathtub. He undressed and sat on the edge of the tub, gazing at the water rising up the white porcelain and thinking of tactics and strategies, supply problems, and the gains made by his Hammerhead Division.

"I'm sure my little pep talks must have had *something* to do with the ground they got last night," he muttered, yawning again and scratching the few gray strands on the top of his head.

At twelve noon, Charlie Company occupied a little hill to the east of Villeruffec, the village they were chased out of two days before. They'd just finished chow and were sitting around smoking cigarettes and talking about the bullshit soldiers talk about when they have free time.

47

"Sheet," said Butsko, lying on the ground with his head resting on his hands and a cigarette dangling out the corner of his mouth. "When this war's over, I'm gonna be sitting pretty. My old man's a shop steward in the big Bethlehem steel mill in my home town, and I'm gonna have me a good job."

"This war ain't ever gonna be over," said Private Pulaski. "It's gonna go on forever."

"The hell it is," Butsko replied. "We got those fucking krauts on the run."

Cranepool sat nearby, ramming a scrap of cloth through the barrel of his M-1. "The Germans have got a lot of fight left in them," he said. "They've had time to rest and regroup. Don't ever count them out until they're out."

"They're out," said Butsko. "Don't worry about it."

Private Riggs sat nearby, his walkie-talkie on his lap. "Sergeant Mahoney said he's gonna open a bar in New York City when this war is over, and he told me I could work for him if I wanted to."

Butsko laughed. "Mahoney would last in the bar business for about a week. He'd drink up all his merchandise by himself. I heard the son of a bitch has got a hollow leg."

"Two hollow legs," Cranepool said.

"Sometimes I think his head is hollow," Butsko said, "but he's got balls of steel."

"He's a crazy son of a bitch," Cranepool agreed.

"Who, me?" Riggs asked.

"Yeah, you're a crazy son of a bitch, too, but he's even crazier than you are, and that's going some."

Riggs pointed. "Here he comes now!"

Everybody looked and saw Mahoney strolling toward them, his carbine slung over his shoulder and a big smile on his face. "Hello there, young warriors," he said cheerfully. "Guess what?"

"What?" everybody asked in unison.

"We're moving back into reserve for a while," he said. "There'll be hot baths and hot chow for everyone. We'll sleep in real beds, and they're even gonna give us a USO show with Bob Hope and Laura Hubbard."

"Laura Hubbard!" they hollered with delight, for she was one of the top stars in Hollywood, right up there with Rita Hayworth and Dorothy Lamour.

"You guys'd better start getting your equipment together,"
Mahoney told them. "If anybody needs me for anything, I'll
be in the latrine jerking off."

Laura Hubbard sat in back of the army bus as it bounced
over the muddy road. She wore GI fatigues, a GI field jacket,
and a GI cap crooked on her head. Her eyes were closed
because she was exhausted from doing two shows a day ever
since she arrived in Europe ten days ago.

In the front of the bus, Bob Hope was cracking jokes with
the driver. He never stopped with the jokes, but Laura felt like
she could sleep for a week, and she was deeply depressed
because the last show had been at a field hospital filled with
mangled young men. She thought it tragic that so many of
them would be maimed and scarred for life, yet they all were
cheerful and overjoyed to see her. She gave them the best
performance she could, although she knew they'd be happy if
she just stood there in her slinky dress for fifteen minutes and
let them look at her. They'd given so much and asked for so
little. She loved them all and wished the war could be over so
they could go home.

The bus bounced so much she couldn't get any rest. With a
sigh, she reached into her field jacket and took out her pack
of cigarettes, lighting one with a gold cigarette lighter given
her by Sam Goldwyn when she'd signed her first contract
with M-G-M. She had auburn hair, brown eyes, and long legs
that had made her a pinup favorite throughout the world. Sam
Goldwyn had told her once that she had the prettiest smile
he'd ever seen, but she suspected he told that to all his stars.
She was twenty-six years old, earned a half million dollars
a year, and managed to spend just about every penny of
it.

Next to Laura sat her hairdresser and makeup artist, Lyle
Farnsworth, whom she'd brought along at her own expense
because she wanted to look her best for America's fighting
men. The rest of the bus was filled with the other members of
the troupe: the magician, puppeteer, and the chorus girls. But
Laura and Bob Hope were the headliners. Bob opened the
show and acted as M.C., and she closed it with her song-and-
dance routine.

Lyle, a gaunt man of fifty wearing a moustache and matching

toupee, pointed out the window. "I believe that's our next stop," he said.

She looked and saw a city of tents and quonset huts spread across a field. It appeared to be deserted. "I wonder where the soldiers are?" she asked.

"Probably at the arena waiting for you, darling."

The bus slowed down, and there was a big commotion as the magician tried to pull down his trunk, filled with tricks, and the chorus girls primped and adjusted their clothes. Bob Hope stood up and did a tap dance in the aisle, singing an old British music-hall tune. Laura turned to Lyle and closed her eyes; he put fresh lipstick on her, powdered her cheeks, and fixed her eyes.

The bus stopped, and the doors opened. Bob Hope was the first one out, holding his right hand straight ahead and grinning like the old showman he was. Colonel Boylan from Special Services was there to shake his hand, and behind Boylan were some members of his staff and a handful of MPs to protect the entertainers from drunk and disorderly GIs.

The entertainers filed off the bus, and when Laura came to the door, she put on her famous smile and stepped down to the mud. She saw all the officers and MPs staring at her, but men had been reacting to her this way since she was sixteen years old. She held out her hand, and Colonel Boylan grasped it, bowing slightly.

"A pleasure to meet you, Miss Hubbard," he said. "Welcome to this camp."

"It's awfully nice to be here," she replied, looking forward at the tents. "I don't see very many soldiers back there. Where are they?"

"The division that was here left this morning for the front, but later in the day the Hammerheads will arrive."

"The Hammerheads?" she asked, pulling a strand of hair back from her eye. "Who are the Hammerheads?"

"Oh," said Boylan, "they're one of the hardest-fighting divisions in the Third Army. The Germans call them 'Roosevelt's Butchers.' We'll have a special MP detachment in front of the stage tonight to protect you from them because they're a wild bunch of boys."

Laura wrinkled her brow and looked at Bob Hope. "I don't

think we need to be protected from American soldiers, do you, Bob?''

''I was just thinking the same thing myself, Laura.'' Bob Hope turned to Colonel Boylan. ''I don't think we want that special detachment of MPs. We don't have anything to fear from our boys in uniform.''

Boylan cleared his throat. ''Maybe you don't, Mister Hope, but I think the ladies might. The Hammerheads are a pretty rowdy bunch, and they've been on the line practically nonstop since D-day. Some of them haven't seen women for a long time. I'd advise you strongly to let us provide this precaution for the ladies in your troupe.''

Laura looked at the chorus girls. ''We're not afraid of American soldiers, are we?''

''Hell, no!'' they said in unison.

Laura turned to the colonel. ''No MPs in front of the stage,'' she said firmly.

''Miss Hubbard, I think you're making a mistake.''

''No MPs,'' she repeated.

Colonel Boylan sighed and shrugged. ''Whatever you say, Miss Hubbard.''

The Hammerheads hit the R & R (rest and recuperation) camp like a hurricane. The first thing they did was invade the PX tent and start swilling down beer. Then they went to the supply tent and drew clean uniforms. The next stop was the latrines so they could shower and shave. The main topic of conversation from one end of the camp to the other was Laura Hubbard and the USO show they were supposed to see that night.

Mahoney finished his shower and stood in front of a mirror, working lather into his black beard with his fingertips. He wore a khaki towel wrapped around his waist and burped from the beer he'd drunk, a little surprised to see his face again and wondering what he'd look like when the beard was gone. The wound on his shoulder was now a thick, dark-red line, but Grossberger had removed the stitches and said it was healing fine.

''Wow,'' said Private, First Class Berman, squeezing his pectoral muscles and rolling his eyes, ''that Laura Hubbard's got tits like two torpedoes. I could swing from them for the rest of my life if she'd let me."

"I'd sell my wife into slavery if I could spend one night with Laura Hubbard!" said Private Trask, sitting on one of the toilets nearby and farting loudly.

Cranepool was shaving the few hairs on his chin. "I can't imagine what it'd be like to go to bed with somebody like her. I'll bet she's just about the best fuck in the world."

Butsko combed his blond hair. "Her kind only fucks millionaires and movie stars."

Mahoney positioned the blade of his razor next to his left sideburn and pulled it down, leaving a swathe of smooth, ruddy skin behind it. "You guys are all a bunch of nitwits," he said. "Any woman can be fucked by any man in the right circumstances. Women like to fuck just like men do, and the prettiest ones like it the most."

Butsko laughed sarcastically. "Tell us about it, sarge."

"Fuck you, twirp," Mahoney replied.

"Mahoney, I heard you ain't had pussy since pussy had you."

"Up your ass with a ten-inch meat hook." Mahoney cleaned the whiskers off his left cheek and then went to work on his right.

"Hey, sarge," said Corporal Shackleton, "what would you do to Laura Hubbard if you ever got alone with her?"

"I'd fuck her deaf, dumb, and blind," Mahoney replied.

Butsko guffawed.

"What would you know about it, Butsko? An asshole like you couldn't get laid in a whorehouse even if you had a fistful of twenties."

"You're all talk and no action, sarge. I mean really—who would want to fuck you?"

"You'd be surprised," Mahoney replied.

"I sure would be. About the only female that would want to fuck you would be a female gorilla."

Butsko laughed, and some of the others laughed with him. Mahoney didn't say anything; he just continued to shave. As his beard slowly was cut away, his facial features began to emerge. He had a few scars on his right cheek where a ricocheting bullet had sent slivers of stone into his flesh.

In a corner, holding his towel and razor, stood Private

Riggs, a scowl on his face. He was all bones and pink skin, and his terrible posture made him look like a hunchback. He didn't like the way Butsko and the others were making fun of Mahoney, who was a hero to him. "I'll bet Sergeant Mahoney could go to bed with Laura Hubbard if he really wanted to," he said in a voice quavering with emotion.

Butsko laughed. "Was that the baboon I just heard talking?"

"Lay off him," Mahoney growled.

"You talk to him that way," Butsko said.

"That's right, but nobody else is gonna talk to him that way."

Butsko frowned as he stepped back from the mirror and let somebody else take his place. He didn't dare to go too far with Mahoney because Mahoney had beat the shit out of him once when Butsko accused Mahoney of cheating in a crap game. But Butsko didn't want to let this new matter drop so easily.

"How much you wanna bet?" Butsko asked Riggs.

"Anything *you* wanna bet," Riggs replied bravely.

"A month's pay?"

"As many months' pay as you want."

"Hey, sarge!" Butsko said loudly. "You've really got this guy trained."

"I said lay off him."

"I'm just trying to make a little bet with him."

"You're just trying to fuck him around, and I told you to cut it out."

"He really thinks you could screw Laura Hubbard if you wanted to. What a dodo bird."

Mahoney turned and looked at Butsko. "I'm not going to tell you again, asshole. Lay off him."

"But you shouldn't let him believe in bullshit things, sarge. You should tell him that you couldn't fuck Laura Hubbard any more than you could fly to the moon."

There was silence for a few moments as Mahoney washed off his razor. Then he bent forward and splashed water on his face, washing away the lather that remained. He pulled the towel from his waist and buried his soaking face in it.

"Who says I can't?" he asked, his voice muffled by the towel.

"Who says you can't what?" Butsko replied.

"Who says I can't fuck Laura Hubbard?" Mahoney said, lowering the towel from his face.

Butsko blinked twice and tried to laugh, but somehow the sound wouldn't rise out of his throat. The latrine became quiet except for the dripping of water. Even Private Trask stopped farting.

"I said you can't," Butsko told Mahoney.

Mahoney stared at him, a cocky smile on his face. "Put your money where your mouth is, shitbird."

Butsko didn't know what to say. How could Mahoney think he could screw the famous glamour queen Laura Hubbard? It simply couldn't be done by a stupid old dogface like him. Was Mahoney trying to trick him? What was going on here?

"You can't be serious," Butsko said with a sneer.

"I've never been more serious in my life," Mahoney replied.

"Come on, sarge, stop pulling my choke."

"I told you I'm serious. How much you wanna bet?"

Butsko glanced around and saw everybody looking at him. He didn't dare back out now. "How much you wanna bet, sarge?"

"How about five hundred dollars?"

"Five hundred dollars!"

"Sure. If I'm gonna go through all the trouble, you gotta make it worth my while."

"Five hundred dollars is a lot of while," Butsko said.

"You didn't think I was going to do it for a month's pay, did you, shitbird? What do you make in a month—twenty dollars? Shove your twenty dollars up your ass. Your old sarge doesn't do anything unless there's big dough involved."

Butsko laughed again because he still thought Mahoney was joking. "Sarge, you almost got me believing that you're serious about this shit."

Mahoney looked Butsko in the eye. "I am serious about it, Butsko. Now put your money where your mouth is or shut the fuck up."

"Where am I gonna get five hundred dollars?" Butsko asked.

"That's your problem. You can owe it to me, or maybe you can give somebody else a piece of the action."

Butsko looked as though he'd seen a ghost. "I think you're serious!"

"You're fucking right I'm serious."

"You really think you can fuck Laura Hubbard!"

"I got five hundred dollars that says I can."

"Show it to me."

Mahoney hesitated because he had only a khaki towel with him. "You got my word."

"Fuck your word. Show me five hundred bananas."

Sgt. Billy McGhee, the mess sergeant for Charlie Company and the biggest wheeler-dealer in the Hammerhead Division, had observed the exchange from a corner of the latrine. He wore a blue terry-cloth robe around his fat torso, and now he stepped forward.

"I'm Mahoney's banker," he said. "I'm backing Mahoney with my own money."

Everybody looked at McGhee. They knew he was a big-time hustler from Philadelphia, and he also was Mahoney's manager and trainer when Mahoney fought in army boxing championships. Mahoney was presently the heavyweight champion of the Hammerhead Division.

"You heard me," McGhee said. "I'm Mahoney's banker." He reached into the pocket of his terry-cloth robe and pulled out a roll of bills thick as his wrist. "How much you want of this, Butsko?"

Butsko was in a daze. Things were moving too fast for him, but he still didn't think Mahoney could screw Laura Hubbard. "Fifty dollars."

McGhee pointed to him. "You're on, peckerhead. Who else?"

Pulaski threw his hands in the air and smiled sheepishly. "Sarge, you know I think a lot of you, but I'm afraid I can't pass this one up." He looked at McGhee. "I'll take fifty, too."

McGhee pointed at him. "You're on!"

"I'll take twenty-five!" yelled Trask.

"I want ten!" cried Berman.

"You're all on!" replied McGhee, pointing at each of them.

Cranepool raised both his hands in the air. "Hold on——I want to put fifty on Mahoney!"

"Me, too!" said Private Grossberger, the medic.

Riggs jumped up and down, "Me, too!"

The rest of the soldiers, regardless of how much they respected Mahoney, all bet against him. They thought he was a great soldier, maybe the greatest in the army, but they didn't see how he could crawl into the bed of the incredible Laura Hubbard. Finally, all the bets were made and covered. The men's faces were flushed with emotion as they moved excitedly about the latrine, pushing each other and waving their arms.

"Hey, wait a minute!" said Butsko. "I just thought of something!" He turned to Mahoney. "If you say you screwed Laura Hubbard, how are we supposed to know you're not lying."

Mahoney balled up his fists. "Are you trying to say I'm a liar?"

"Well, I saw you pull a fast one with a pair of dice once."

Mahoney lunged at Butsko, but big fat Sergeant McGhee got between them and held Mahoney back. Cranepool grabbed one of Mahoney's arms.

"Cool down, sarge," Cranepool said.

Private Berman raised his finger in the air. "Butsko's got a point," he said. "There's a lot of dough involved here. How are we supposed to know whether or not you screw this cunt?"

Mahoney calmed down because he realized that Butsko and Berman were right. "I'll tell you what," he said. "I'll bring you back her draws. Will that be good enough?"

Butsko nodded. "You bring back her draws and that'll be good enough for me."

"Me, too," said Berman, "and I hope they smell sweet."

Mahoney grunted. "I'll bet they smell sweeter than your breath, fuckhead."

He walked to one of the hooks on the wall and took down his freshly laundered fatigues. Now the excitement was over, and the men continued shaving and taking showers. Private Trask felt free to fart again. The latrine coalesced into groups of men talking about the bets they'd just made. McGhee, Cranepool, Grossberger, and Riggs huddled around Mahoney.

McGhee shook his head. "I must have been out of my mind to back you on this one," he said.

"Why did you?" Mahoney asked.

"I don't know. I guess I thought you could do it."

"I thought I could, too." Mahoney sighed.

"What! You mean you don't think you can now!"

"It isn't going to be easy. I guess I got caught up in the excitement there. That goddamn Butsko always manages to piss me off."

Cranepool patted Mahoney on the shoulder. "You can do it, sarge."

"Yeah," said Riggs, his eyes popping out of his head.

"You've done harder things," Grossberger added.

Mahoney buttoned on his fatigue shirt. "Well, I suppose where there's a will, there's a way."

The entertainers dined that evening in the officers' mess, which was a big quonset hut. They split up and sat at tables with officers, and Laura Hubbard wound up with General Donovan and Colonel Boylan. The two officers tried to behave like gentlemen, but Laura was amused to notice that their eyes were drawn repeatedly to her famous bosom, and she realized that they hadn't seen their wives for a long time, and they must be horny as a pair of old billy goats. The conversation was beginning to lag, because the officers and Laura lived in very different worlds, but she didn't want to make them feel uncomfortable, so she thought she'd say something to keep the patter going.

She turned to General Donovan. "I understand the Germans call your division 'Roosevelt's Butchers.'"

Donovan blushed. "Why, yes, they do. I think it's rather unfortunate myself because they're good soldiers and not bloodthirsty killers as the term indicates."

"How long have they been fighting here."

"They hit Omaha Beach on D-day, and they've been here ever since."

"That's a long time," Laura said.

"Yes, it has, but of course some of the men have been in the war much longer than that. Some of them have fought since the very beginning in North Africa."

"They must be very brave men."

"The bravest," Donovan agreed. "Sometimes they get a little out of hand, but nobody can say they're not brave." He looked up at her from his beef stew. "Colonel Boylan here told me that you refused to have MP protection during the show tonight. It's very nice of you to have that kind of faith in our boys, and I appreciate your sentiments, but these boys have been out in the front lines for a long time, and I don't think they're very civilized right now. If I looked the way you looked"—and here he lowered his eyes—"I don't think I'd want to get on the stage without a cordon of MPs in front of me."

"Don't worry about it, general," she said confidently. "I can handle them."

Donovan sighed. "I certainly hope so."

The table became silent again. Laura raised a spoonful of beef stew to her mouth and saw a handsome young lieutenant looking at her from another table. She averted his glance quickly because the last thing she needed was to get mixed up with some soldier while she was on a USO show. That sort of thing would look awfully bad in the papers, although she wouldn't mind getting mixed up with a nice-looking young soldier for a little while. She was a wild young thing and was accustomed to steady nooky, but she presently was going through her fourth divorce and hadn't had any nooky for over a month. Sometimes, surrounded by strapping young soldiers, she got a little itchy and scratchy, but she intended to hold out until she got back to Hollywood.

"Where are you from, general?" she asked.

"Atlanta," he replied.

"Nice town."

"Yes."

She continued to exchange pleasantries with the officers, wishing the show was over so she could go to bed. She also wished she could have a drink, but that also was off limits to her while she was on the USO tour.

Well, she thought philosophically, *we all have to give up something for the war effort, I suppose.*

EIGHT

It was night, and the rain had stopped. The men and officers of the Hammerhead Division were gathered around the stage, waiting for the show to begin. They sat or kneeled on the ground, which they'd covered first with their ponchos, and spoke of Laura Hubbard and the chorus girls. The band was tuning up in front of the stage, which was a raised wooden platform protected from the rain by a tarpaulin. Behind the stage were eight squad tents that served as dressing rooms for the entertainers.

"Hey, when's the fucking show gonna start!" somebody shouted.

"Bring on the girls!"

"Where's Laura Hubbard! Tell her to get her little ass out here!"

The men had been drinking PX beer all day, and many couldn't even see the stage. In the first platoon of Charlie Company, Butsko sat with his buddies and wore a worried frown on his face because he didn't see Mahoney around. Butsko still firmly believed that Mahoney never in a million years could seduce Laura Hubbard, but in a tiny cranny of Butsko's brain he entertained the possibility that Mahoney actually might do it, for he knew that he had done all sorts of impossible things on the battlefield and might actually pull this one off.

"Anybody see Mahoney?" he asked.

"Naw," said Berman. "Wonder where the son of a bitch is?"

Sergeant McGhee chortled. "He's probably got his dick up Larua Hubbard's ass right now."

"Boolshit," said Butsko.

"You'd better say good-by to your fifty bucks, asshole."

59

"We'll see about that, McGhee."

"*Sergeant* McGhee to you, fucknose."

Suddenly the spotlight lit up the stage, and the band began to play Bob Hope's theme song "Thanks for the Memory." The GIs jumped up and clapped their hands wildly as Bob Hope climbed on to the stage wearing baggy fatigues with a steel helmet on backwards and proceeded to the microphone, holding both of his hands out to the side and smiling from ear to ear. He tried to talk, but the applause was too loud. As he paused, holding his hands out to make them quiet down, they only applauded louder. They knew he came all the way from the States to see them, and they wanted him to know they appreciated it.

Bob Hope stood at the microphone, and tears came to his eyes. He bowed once and bowed again, but still they kept on applauding. He looked at his watch and made a funny face, but they continued to applaud. Then he did a pratfall and rolled toward the edge of the stage.

The GIs stopped clapping and held their breaths, wondering if he'd fall off the stage, but he back-flipped neatly to his feet and leaned toward the microphone.

"I knew that one would quiet you down," he said with a wink.

They applauded and screamed again, this time louder than before. Bob Hope leaned his arm on the microphone and decided to wait until they calmed down. *They said the Hammerheads are a little wild,* he thought, *and I guess they weren't kidding.*

Mahoney marched smartly toward the quonset-hut area where the entertainers would spend the night. He wore a plain fatigue shirt with the insignia of a major on his collar plus an MP armband around his sleeve. Around his waist was a cartridge belt with an officers's Colt .45 hanging from it. He also had a major's oak leaf on his helmet liner.

Hoping he wouldn't run into anybody he knew, he made his way to the quonset hut in which Laura Hubbard would spend the night. A private, first class in the MPs was standing at a stiff parade rest in front of it, and Mahoney marched toward him, frowning the way officers often frown when approaching a hapless enlisted man. When the private first class saw him, he snapped to attention and saluted. Mahoney returned the salute and looked the private first class up and down.

"What's your name, soldier?" Mahoney asked.

"Pfc. Olivero, sir."

"Everything under control?"

"Yes, sir."

Mahoney examined Olivero's face. "Did you shave before you came on duty tonight, Olivero?"

"Yes, sir!"

"Doesn't look it to me!"

"I did, sir!"

Mahoney harumphed. "Let me see your weapon."

The private, first class brought his carbine around and opened the bolt smartly. Mahoney took it from him, turned around, and looked down the barrel, dropping some dirt surreptitiously in the chamber as he did so.

"This weapon is filthy, soldier!" Mahoney bellowed.

"But I cleaned it just before I came on duty, sir!"

Mahoney held up the carbine. "You call this clean?"

The MP looked into the chamber and went pale. "No, sir," he said weakly.

"I think you'd better clean it *right now!*"

"Right now, sir?"

"Are your ears filthy, too, soldier? Are they all clogged up with dirt?"

"No, sir."

"Then take this weapon back to your tent and clean it immediately!"

"But, sir!" protested the MP, "who'll guard this quonset hut?"

"Don't worry about it," Mahoney snarled. "Nobody's here now, anyway. You'll be back before the person to whom this hut is assigned shows up. I can't have you standing guard with a filthy weapon. Now get going!"

"Yes, sir!"

"On the double!"

"Yes, sir!"

The MP ran off, and Mahoney smiled slightly, waiting until he was out of sight. Then Mahoney bent toward the door and inserted a pick that McGhee had made out of the tine of a fork. Mahoney had picked a few locks in his day back in New

York during the Depression. A person had to get money somehow in those days, and he hadn't been able to find a job.

The lock in the door snapped. Mahoney turned the knob and entered the quonset hut, pulling the door closed behind him and locking it again. It was dark in the quonset hut, and he smelled perfume. His eyes adjusted quickly, and he could see women's garments lying around. He knew he could find a pair of Laura Hubbard's underpants and bring them back to the first platoon to win his bet, but that would be cheating, and Mahoney wasn't a cheater. He wanted to win his money fair and square, and he was willing to go for broke. Looking at his watch, he figured that the show would last about two more hours.

The soldiers finally quieted down, and Bob Hope told a few ribald jokes that he'd never get away with on his radio show in the States. The soldiers, starved for entertainment, howled with laughter and clapped their hands. Then Bob Hope told a few more jokes, and the troops began to get restless, for although they liked to laugh, they'd much rather see females.

One of the soldiers stood up, cupped his hands around his mouth, and shouted: "Bring on the girls!"

"Yeah!" yelled another. "Where are the girls!"

"Get the girls out here!"

"We want girls!"

Bob Hope had worked hundreds of USO shows, and he knew how to handle the soldiers. "What did you say you wanted?" he asked, cupping a hand behind his ear.

"Girls!"

"What was that?"

"Girls!"

"Did you say girls?"

"Yeah!"

Bob Hope turned and held the palm of his hand out to the quonset huts behind him, and the chorus girls came out of a door. They wore skimpy red, white, and blue costumes and climbed on to the stage as the soldiers screamed at the tops of their lungs and threw their hats in the air. The girls formed a chorus line, and the band struck up a tune. The girls sang and danced, wiggling their boobs and behinds and acting as naughty as they dared, considering the circumstances.

The soldiers cheered so loudly they couldn't hear the band or the girl's voices. The men slobbered and drooled, and an unseen force caused them to press closer to the stage. Bob Hope saw them coming and realized they looked like a desperate bunch. He began to wonder if it might not have been a good idea to have the MP cordon for protection. The soldiers pressed against the stage and reached toward the girls, begging them to come closer, making disgusting sexual remarks. Although some of the girls wanted to run and hide, they all kicked their legs and sang their little song, just as they always did.

Corporal Butsko, his fingernails clawing the top of the stage, looked into the crotches of the dancing girls and thought the top of his head would blow off. He wanted to rush up there and nuzzle his nose between the legs of the redhead in front of him and then throw her down and ravish her. But he stayed where he was and gazed at her longingly; he knew that if he put one foot on the stage, he'd wind up in the stockade so fast he wouldn't know what hit him.

It was the same way with the other GIs; they all were afraid of court-martial tribunals and stockades. Many of them already had served time in stockades, and the experience had shattered them for life. They would charge enemy tanks singlehandedly, but they were afraid of being thrown back into a stockade.

The girls shook their fannies in front of the men's faces, and the soldiers screamed at the tops of their lungs, but not one of them ventured on to the stage. They pounded their fists on the planks of the stage and ogled the girls shamelessly, but that was as far as they dared to go.

The girls finished their act and danced off the stage, but the soldiers hollered so loudly they had to return for two encores. After that, they ran out of material, so they left the stage for the time being, although the soldiers shook the stage and screamed like hyenas.

The next act was the magician and his lady assistant, and the GIs fastened their eyes on the lady assistant, not giving a damn whether the magician pulled the rabbit out of his hat or not. Every time she moved, they cheered, and whenever she bent over, they made obscene sounds, while the magician valiantly made cards disappear and pulled hard-boiled eggs out of the thin air.

The magic act was followed by a comedy routine in which Bob Hope played a soldier who'd been assigned to a WAC detachment by mistake. The WACs were played by various chorus girls, who wore skirts much shorter than those worn by real WACs, and it was all so ridiculous and funny that the GIs couldn't help laughing uproariously. The tension and anxiety of the past weeks exploded out of them, and the wonderful release made them feel euphoric. Somehow all the suffering and danger seemed worth it to them now because they knew somebody cared about them enough to come to where they were and put on this great show. They laughed without restraint at corny and stupid jokes, and perhaps Bob Hope was led to believe that he was a greater comedian than he actually was, but the moments were magic ones, and a good time was had by all.

Finally, the comedy routine ended, and Bob Hope took his bows in front of the girls who'd assisted him. The soldiers pounded their hands together and blew kisses at the girls, who returned to their dressing rooms, leaving Bob Hope alone in front of the microphone.

"Well, boys," he said, "our next act is supposed to be Laura Hubbard, but—"

He was unable to finish the sentence because the soldiers began cheering loudly. This was the moment they were waiting for, the high point of the show. Every one of them knew who Laura Hubbard was, and every one of them at some time in his life had dreamed of making love to her. Now they were going to see her alive in person and in the flesh. To them it was an event nearly comparable to the Second Coming of Christ.

Bob Hope held his hands up, indicating that they should quiet down, and they realized that Laura Hubbard wouldn't come out unless they shut up, so gradually the cheering died down, and the men stood on their tiptoes, their eyes glued on the stage and their faces expressing the anticipation of something wonderful.

"As I was saying," Bob Hope continued, "our next act was supposed to be Laura Hubbard, but she told me a little while ago that she thought you fellers really didn't want to see her and that you'd rather see Lana Turner or Marlene Dietrich or somebody like that. I told her she was wrong, but she didn't believe me." He pointed to the quonset huts behind him. "She's right back there right now, but she's not coming out here unless she's convinced that you really want to see her, so what do you say, guys, do you really want to see her?"

Pandemonium broke out among the soldiers. Although they knew he was bullshitting them, they were willing to play along. They shouted at the tops of their lungs and clapped their hands. The ones close to the stage pounded their helmets on it. Bob Hope stood at the microphone and felt the stage shaking underneath his feet. He used that same routine before every audience on his USO tour, but he'd never seen a response like this. Now he realized why the Germans called these men "Roosevelt's Butchers." If they brought that same emotion to the front lines, they would have to be unstoppable.

The lights went out, plunging the stage into darkness. Some of the soldiers became frightened, thinking they'd broken the electrical connections. They moved around restlessly, wondering what was going on.

Then they heard the voice of Bob Hope on the microphone: "And now, the girl you've all been waiting for, the exquisite Laura Hubbard!"

A single spotlight came on, and in its center was Laura Hubbard, standing beside the microphone. She wore a white gown slit up the left leg and covered with rhinestones that glittered in the light. The dress was cut low in front and hugged her curvaceous body like a second skin. She looked unreal, like the vision of female perfection that each of them carried in his mind, and there she was, in front of them, alive and smiling, taking a bow.

At first, the soldiers were struck dumb. They stared at her, their jaws agape, and couldn't believe she was really there. She was so beautiful and so different from their wives and sweethearts and kid sisters that she seemed like a different species of female. The band began to play, and she held out her arms to them, winking and moving her hips from side to side to the rhythm of the music. She opened her mouth and sang.

The soldiers came back to their senses and cheered. They shook their heads and bellowed like wild animals. Clapping their hands high in the air, they drowned out her voice and the band, but they couldn't control themselves. Their eyes glazed with madness, they threw all caution to the wind and began to climb on to the stage.

Bob Hope held out his hands and walked toward them. "Now boys," he said.

But they couldn't hear him and didn't give a damn, anyway. Machine guns couldn't keep them off the stage now, and they didn't care about courts-martial and stockades. They scrambled on to the stage and rushed toward Laura Hubbard.

She saw them coming and didn't flinch. After years as one of Hollywood's top stars, she'd become so vain she thought she was invincible. She just kept on singing, rolling her eyes and shaking her hips. GIs crowded on to the stage and surrounded her, inching closer, their eyes bulging and tongues hanging out of their mouths. "I'm feeling sad and lonely, lonely, as I can be."

She removed the microphone from the stand and strolled toward them. They couldn't believe their eyes and stopped dead in their tracks. Her confidence and magical aura was too much for them. She ran the palm of her hand over the crew cut of a nineteen-year-old private who'd once charged a tank with only his M-1 rifle, and he nearly fainted from the thrill of her touch. She patted the chin of an old sergeant who was a known bayonet killer, and he smiled like a little boy. Still singing and carrying her microphone, she moved from soldier to soldier, winking at them and touching them, shaking her hips and almost daring them to get out of line, but they made no move to touch her and only looked at her worshipfully, being transported to a heavenly place where there was no war and no brutality, where only beauty and rapture existed, and where no one would ever die.

NINE

At ten o'clock in the evening, General Donovan and a group of staff officers escorted Laura back to the quonset hut where she'd spend the night. The rain fell lightly, and she wore an army field jacket over her glittering dress. Two young lieutenants held a poncho over her head so she wouldn't get wet.

"It was a wonderful show," General Donovan said enthusiastically. "Just what the men needed. You were great, just great. You had them all in the palm of your hand, and me, too, I must confess."

"I enjoyed every minute of it," Laura replied with a gay toss of her head. "There's nothing like a real audience to make a performer feel alive."

Some of the officers thought Laura said those things only to be polite, but she was telling the truth. She'd been invigorated by the show and the excitement she'd produced in the soldiers. It had been similar when she'd been a stage actress; she'd had more energy after a performance than before it. If she were in Hollywood right now, she'd go out and party all night long, but there was no place to party here. All she could do was go to bed, and in the morning she'd travel with the troupe to the next camp and the next show. In a week, she'd return to the States, and maybe President Roosevelt would give her a medal.

The officers continued to praise her as they walked in the paths between tents, and finally they came to her quonset hut. It normally was used for visiting dignitaries such as General Patton when he happened to be in the area, and tonight it would be hers. The MP standing guard in front of it snapped to attention as she approached with the officers, and he saluted General Donovan.

"At ease," said Donovan, saluting him back.

The MP moved to parade rest, and General Donovan turned to Laura.

"Well, good night," he said.

"Good night," she replied. "By the way, I really don't need that MP standing here all night, do I?"

"Well, it's for your own security, Miss Hubbard."

"I'd feel just as secure without him, and, in fact, I'd feel uncomfortable knowing someone was standing outside my door all night. Can't you dismiss him?"

"Well, if you'd like me to, Miss Hubbard."

"I'd like you to very much."

General Donovan looked at the MP. "Report to the provost marshal and tell him I've relieved you of duty for the night."

The MP drew himself to attention and smiled. "Yes, sir!" He saluted and marched off.

The officers wished Laura a good night and thanked her again for her magnificent performance. Finally, she opened the door to her quonset hut, and the officers moved away.

She stepped inside the hut, turned on the light switch, and closed the door. She saw her cot, the trunk she traveled with, and a little dressing table that had thoughtfully been set up for her. An enclosed shower room and toilet were at the far end of the hut, and it all looked bleak and grim to her, a far cry from her luxurious home in Beverly Hills.

She took off her field jacket and hung it on the peg near the door. A kerosene stove was in the center of the hut, making it cozy and warm. She walked toward it, holding out her hands to warm them, wondering what to do with herself because she didn't feel like going to bed yet. She'd brought a book along, *Requiem for a Nun* by William Faulkner, and she thought she might read part of it. Sam Goldwyn had writers working on the script, and it was rumored that she might get the female lead.

"Don't get scared," said a male voice.

She turned around sharply and saw in a shadowy corner a big brawny soldier wearing officers' insignia on his collar. At first, she became frightened, but he made no menacing moves.

"What are you doing here!" she demanded.

He smiled as he stepped toward her. "I figured you might

like to have a little drink after the show.'' Reaching into his back pocket, Mahoney took out McGhee's silver flask. ''I got a little cognac here that's very good. It was liberated from the headquarters of a German general.''

She stared at him and wondered what was going on. ''Who are you?'' she asked.

''My name's Mahoney. I'm a platoon sergeant in the Fifteenth Regiment.'' He touched the officer's insignia on his collar. ''I wore this just to get in here.''

Laura now wished she hadn't dismissed that MP. ''You must be crazy to break in here like this,'' she said, getting frightened.

He noticed her fear. ''I'll leave if you want me to.'' He held out the flask. ''You can have this as a present. It's terrific stuff, and it was all I could do to keep from drinking it all up while I was waiting.''

She looked him up and down and thought he resembled John Garfield, whom she knew rather well. But his features were cruder than John's, and he was much bigger than John, too. She noticed the little scars on his cheek and wondered where he got them. His shirt fit him tightly, and she could perceive his bulging muscles and flat stomach.

She still didn't know what to do. ''You've got a lot of guts to break in here like this, soldier.''

''Compared to what?''

She looked again at the scars on his cheek, feeling foolish. He'd probably done much more dangerous things than sneak into a woman's bedroom. If he was going to rape her, he wouldn't just be standing there looking ill at ease.

''I don't know what to do about you,'' she said. ''I wouldn't want to call the MPs and get you into trouble.''

He unscrewed the top of the flask. ''Why don't you have a drink with me?''

She looked at him and his flask and admitted to herself that she really didn't feel very tired. He looked like an interesting guy, and he wasn't bad-looking at all.

''All right,'' she said. ''What the hell?''

''That's the spirit,'' he replied. ''Do you have any glasses, or should we drink out of the bottle?''

''I don't know what I've got here. I guess we can drink

right out of the bottle. Why don't you bring that chair up, and I'll sit on the cot.''

Mahoney moved swiftly to the dressing table, picked up the chair in front of it, and placed it beside the cot. Laura sat on the cot and propped the pillow against the wall so she could lean back. She crossed her legs and noticed Mahoney looking at the flesh that the slit in her dress had uncovered.

"You're not going to do anything crazy, are you?" she asked.

"Like what?" he replied, unscrewing the cap from the flask.

"You know."

He smiled, and his straight teeth gleamed in the light of the electric lamp. She realized that his nose was slightly out of line; it must have been broken someplace.

"I'm not going to attack you if that's what you mean," he said.

"That's what I mean."

"Relax and have a drink."

He held out the flask, and she took it from his big gnarled hand. Raising it to her lips, she took a swig. As it went down, she realized he'd been telling the truth; it was superb cognac. She handed it back, and he had a drink, his Adam's apple bobbing up and down. They passed the flask back and forth a few times, and everything got mellow. Mahoney took out a package of Chesterfields and offered her one. He lit her cigarette, then one for himself. They looked at each other through the smoky haze.

"How was the show?" he asked.

"You weren't there?"

"I was here."

She puffed the cigarette. "It was a fabulous show. The men in the division are really something. You've all got quite a reputation."

"What kind of reputation?"

"You're supposed to be great soldiers."

Mahoney shrugged. "Who the hell knows?"

"Where are you from?" she asked.

"New York City."

"What did you do before the war?"

"I was in the army before the war," Mahoney answered. "I'm a career soldier." He held up the flask. "Have another drink."

She took the flask and drank some more. "I haven't done anything like this since I was a kid."

Mahoney chortled. "Shit, you're still a kid." He lifted the bottle from her fingers.

She became annoyed because she wasn't accustomed to being spoken to that way. "I'm not a kid," she said testily.

"Sure you are. You can't be much more than twenty." He raised the flask to his lips.

She didn't want to be drawn into an argument over her age, so she kept her mouth shut and became more annoyed.

"Calm down," he said.

"I'm calm."

"No, you're not. Have another drink." He held up the flask.

"I don't want another drink."

"C'mon, don't be mad at me," he said. "I'm just a crazy old soldier boy. Here—have another drink."

She looked at him and could sense his powerful masculine presence. He was starting to turn her on. She'd always been attracted, in spite of herself, to tough guys. "Well, maybe just one more," she said.

She took the flask and drank a few sips, gazing at him through heavily lidded eyes. He puffed his cigarette and smiled faintly. The more she drank, the better he looked. And she hadn't had any nooky for a month.

"You know," Mahoney said, "you're even prettier in real life than you are in the movies."

"I suppose," she replied dryly, "that I'm not so bad for a kid."

"Well," he said, trying to make amends, "compared to me, you're a kid, but compared to kids, you're no kid."

She took a drag on her cigarette. "I really don't know what I'm doing here with you."

"Relax and don't worry about it."

"They'll probably put you before a firing squad if they find you here."

"Probably."

"Don't you care?"

"I'll probably be killed before long, anyways, so what does it matter?"

She looked at the scars on his face, and the reality of the situation broke through to her. He was a front-line combat soldier in an outfit the Germans called "Roosevelt's Butchers." He wasn't John Wayne pretending to be a soldier in a movie; he was a real soldier, and he might not survive the war.

"You poor bastard," she said softly.

He was surprised by her sudden change of mood. "What are you talking about?"

"Never mind. Can I have another drink?"

"Sure."

He passed her the flask, and she drank some more. The cognac was getting to her, and she felt a little weird.

"You know," she said, "you're charming in a certain strange way."

"So are you," he replied with a grin.

"You've got a lot of guts coming here like this."

"Cut that shit out, will you?"

She laughed. "Did you really think you could seduce me?"

"I don't know what I thought. I guess I just wanted to give it a try. What the hell?"

She rubbed the mouth of the bottle against her lips, thinking he had a very sexy body. "I'm glad you came here," she told him.

"I'm glad I did, too," he replied. "You're a sight for my tired old eyes, let me tell you."

"You're the kind of man that women like, and you know it, don't you?"

He shrugged. "I suppose I do."

'You know that if you can get alone with a woman, she probably wouldn't resist you very much."

"Some have."

Her eyes became sultry. "I wouldn't."

Mahoney rose from the chair, moved toward her, took her shoulders in his hands, and gently moved her sideways until she was lying on the cot. Then he lay beside her, hugged her to him, and kissed her lips. She opened her mouth, and their tongues entwined. *I can't believe it*, Mahoney thought. *I'm actually kissing Laura Hubbard.*

Her lips tasted like raspberries, and her body was sinuous and quivering. He was afraid she'd come to her senses and stop him, so he pulled her to him more firmly, and probed her mouth with his tongue. Her fingernails scratched the back of his shirt and she made a soft whimpering sound that was her declaration of surrender. Her perfume assailed him like the smoke of opium, and he felt the world spinning around.

He reached to her knee and caressed the smooth skin encased in silk stocking. Running his hand up her thigh, he felt the temperature become warmer. He touched her lace underpants, and made a quick decision not to grab her treasure too soon and scare her, so he placed the palm of his hand against her famous rear end, and pulled her closer to his flaming erection.

She squirmed and moaned. Raising her hands to his cheeks, she pushed him away.

"Look at me," she said.

"I'm looking at you."

"I mean eye to eye."

"Okay."

Their eyes met, and he thought hers were pools in the moonlight.

"Mahoney," she said, "you're not going to kiss and tell are you?"

"What do you mean?"

"You know what I mean. You're not going to tell all your buddies, are you?"

"I wouldn't do that," Mahoney said.

"I hope not because that kind of talk would get around, and it wouldn't be good for me. I'm married, you know."

"I know."

"Look me in the eye and promise me you won't say anything to anybody no matter what."

Mahoney sighed. "I won't say anything to anybody no matter what."

"Cross your heart and hope to die."

"Come on," Mahoney said.

"I mean it."

"Cross my heart and hope to die," he said, tracing his forefinger over the spot where he thought his heart was.

"Thank you," she said, kissing his cheek. "And now there's one more thing I want to ask you. Would you unzip the back of my dress for me, please?"

TEN

There was no reveille the next morning, and the soldiers were permitted to sleep as late as they wanted. Around eleven o'clock, the men from the first platoon gathered in front of the squad tent where Mahoney was snoring away.

"Did he do it?" Private, First Class Berman asked.

Butsko grimaced and waved his hand in the air. "Don't be an asshole. Of course he didn't do it. If he did, he would have come right to my tent and thrown Linda Hubbard's draws in my face."

"Maybe so," Cranepool said, "but he didn't get in until 0400 hours this morning."

"What!" said Butsko.

"That's right. I sleep in the same squad tent, and I was aware when he came back."

Butsko granted. "So he was out late, so what? He was probably jerking off in the woods someplace. He didn't screw Laura Hubbard. He's so full of shit it's starting to come out of his ears."

Cranepool narrowed his eyes at Butsko. "That ain't no way to talk about Mahoney."

Butsko spat into the mud. "Fuck him and fuck you."

Cranepool made a threatening motion toward Butsko, and Butsko made fists.

"What's going on here?" asked big fat Sergeant McGhee, strolling up to them. "Did he or didn't he?"

Butsko laughed sarcastically. "Are you fucking kidding me? Of course he didn't."

"You don't know that," Cranepool said.

"What a bunch of clowns you guys are," Butsko said. "You actually believe he could do it."

McGhee looked toward the squad tent, from which issued the snores of Mahoney. "What has he had to say?"

"He hasn't said anything," Cranepool replied. "He got in at 0400 hours and collapsed into bed."

McGhee smiled. "Really?"

"Yeah."

"Let's wake the fucker up and ask him."

"But he's asleep."

"He's slept long enough."

McGhee pushed aside the flap and entered the tent, the whole platoon following him in. Mahoney lay on his belly with his face sideways on the pillow, his mouth open and one hand near his chin. McGhee reached down and grabbed Mahoney's bicep, shaking him from side to side.

"Wake up and piss," McGhee said, "the world's on fire!"

Mahoney lunged up, his teeth bared like an animal and his hands going for McGhee's throat.

McGhee stepped backward. "Hey, cool your motor, Mahoney."

Mahoney looked around and saw the platoon. He groaned as he realized what they wanted.

"Well," McGhee said, "have you got her draws?"

Mahoney shook his head and looked forlornly into his lap. "No."

Butsko jumped into the air and cheered. "I told you he couldn't do it!" He charged toward Mahoney and held the palm of his hand underneath Mahoney's nose. "Pay up, sarge!"

Mahoney looked at McGhee. "I'll make it up to you. Don't worry."

McGhee was disappointed because he thought Mahoney really could do what he said. The soldiers looked at Mahoney, and some of them felt sad. Mahoney took his pack of cigarettes out of his combat boots and appeared to be completely demoralized. The men had never seen him looking so unhappy. Riggs reached down and lit his cigarette.

"It's okay, sarge," Riggs said. "Don't worry about it."

Berman held out his hands and smiled. "Hey, what's everybody so serious about here? This whole thing's supposed to be a joke, isn't it? I mean, you guys really didn't expect Mahoney to screw that broad, did you? How in the hell could he do that? Are you guys kidding?"

Butsko shook his head. "I wasn't kidding. I made a bet with him, and I think he should pay up."

"Come off it, Butsko," Berman said.

"Yeah," added Private, First Class Stafford. "Get serious. How could Mahoney screw that broad. She probably was surrounded by a detachment of MPs even when she went to the latrine."

Butsko shrugged. "That's was Mahoney's problem, not mine."

"Hey, Butsko," said Private Trask. "Don't be such a fucking hump all your life, hump."

"Hump your mother's pussy," Butsko retorted. "I made a bet, and I want my money."

Mahoney puffed his cigarette. "Everybody'll get paid," he said.

Butsko looked at Mahoney. "You really had a lot of these guys fooled, sarge. But you can't fool old Butsko."

"Well," Mahoney said, his eyes downcast, "I guess I had a few beers too many when I made that bet."

"Aw shit," said Pulaski, "we all had a few beers too many. I can't take Mahoney's money. I mean, how could he fuck Laura Hubbard? Even God couldn't do that."

"God could do anything," Riggs said.

"Shaddup asshole."

"I don't give a shit," Butsko said. "I want my dough."

McGhee took his roll out of his pocket. "You got it," he said, peeling off two twenties and a ten.

Butsko took the money and turned around. "What's the matter with you fucking guys! You made a bet, didn't you?"

"It wasn't a real bet," Trask said.

"Yeah," added Stafford, "you're the only one who took it seriously."

"Sheet," said Butsko, "if he woulda come back with her draws, then it woulda been a bet."

"How could he come back with her draws?"

Butsko pinched his lips together, getting angry. He was the only one holding Mahoney to the bet, and that made him look bad. Moreover, Mahoney was his platoon sergeant and could make his life miserable, maybe even get him killed.

"Aw shit!" he sid, throwing the money into the air and storming out of the tent. "Fuck all you guys."

Riggs bent down and picked up the money, giving it to McGhee. Everybody looked at Mahoney, who was sitting on his cot, inhaling his cigarette.

"What do you guys think this is," Mahoney said, "a fucking zoo?"

The men shuffled out of the tent. Mahoney pushed his covers back and planted his feet on the floor. He whistled a tune as he walked to his foot locker and took out his fatigue pants.

ELEVEN

After a week on R & R, the Hammerhead Division was returned to the line in the Moselle sector. They had little gas and ammunition and could only conduct limited objective attacks to improve local positions.

The Hammerheads and the rest of the Third Army were kept on a leash throughout October, while Field Marshal Montgomery's Twenty-First British Army Group tried to clear the port of Antwerp and General Hodges' First U.S. Army was stalled at Aachen.

It was a difficult period for General Patton, who was anxious to get rolling again. He toured his lines incessantly, trying to encourage his men and keep their morale high, and in the evenings he studied maps to determine his next moves because it was anticipated that the supply shortage would end in the early part of November.

But deep in his heart he was more demoralized than anyone, for he knew that a golden opportunity had slipped through his fingers. He knew that if he had the supplies he needed, he could have pushed onward to the Siegfried Line, crashed through it, and charged unopposed toward Berlin. He could have ended the war in two weeks, but now the Germans were building up their forces in front of him, and when he resumed his offensive, he could expect heavy casualties. Many American soldiers would die because of Ike's inability to understand the realities of the front and because of General Montgomery's arrogance.

In the presence of his men and officers, General Patton strutted about with his riding crop and pearl-handled revolver, exuding confidence and bestowing medals on soldiers who'd distinguished themselves in battle. He couldn't let them see his frustration and pain.

A general is just a cheerleader, he said to himself late one night as he was preparing for bed. Without his helmet and shirt, stripped of his polished boots and fancy riding jodhpurs, he looked like a bald old man with bad teeth and a potbelly. He was fifty-nine years old and had a premonition that he would not live much longer. He was certain he could win the war if they'd just let him, but they wouldn't let him.

Before retiring for the night, he kneeled beside his bed and prayed that God would give him the strength to carry on.

TWELVE

Opposite Patton's Third Army was the German *Armeegruppe G*, commanded by Gen. Hermann Balck, a blond, blue-eyed, gentle-looking man who in reality was a fierce soldier and a dedicated follower of Adolf Hitler.

One morning toward the end of October, he held a meeting with his staff officers in a former schoolhouse not far from the front. They gathered around the map table, and General Balck stood with his hands behind his back looking instensely pleased with himself. He was a vain, conceited man and had been appointed to his command personally by Adolf Hitler, whose portrait hung on a wall of the conference room.

"Well, gentlemen," he said, gazing down at the map, "it's been quite a month. Never in my career have I commanded such motley and badly equipped troops, and yet we succeeded in stopping the great General Patton." Balck chortled. "It appears that this General Patton isn't as great as he thinks he is. We have all seen that he is a timid leader, unable to exploit the very considerable opportunities that lay before him at the beginning of this month, for as we all know, there was nothing between him and the heart of Germany. Of course, he's made some small, insignificant gains during this period, but that was to be expected given his overwhelming superiority in numbers of troops and quantities of material. Yet how amazing it is that we, with only hastily formed units, comprised of old men and teenaged boys, of cooks and bakers and file clerks, could stop his much-vaunted army and consolidate our own lines." Balck pointed to the map. "We can't say for sure where he'll make his next effort, but we can expect that he'll try something soon. Therefore, my orders to you are that we must hold fast and not give up any ground whatsoever. That is what the *Fuehrer* requests, and that is what we shall do. I repeat: *We shall not give up any ground whatsoever.* Are there any questions?''

No one ventured to raise his hand or say anything.

''Very well,'' Balck said. ''I would like to leave all of you with this last thought. The German soldier is a superior soldier. One German soldier is worth ten American soldiers. The crisis we faced at the beginning of this month is over, and we now have a stable line and new troops. If there are any failures to hold our positions, local commanders will be held personally responsible because there can be no excuses for failure now. Let me tell you, gentlemen, that I would hate to be in the shoes of any officer who fails to do his duty. Do I make myself clear?''

The officers nodded or muttered that they understood.

Balck smiled faintly. ''This meeting if over,'' he said. ''Heil Hitler!''

Mahoney sat in a foxhole, eating C rations in the rain. He wore his helmet and poncho, hadn't shaved for three days, and had a mild case of trenchfoot. He and the rest of Charlie Company had been in this desolate sector of the front since returning from R & R, and hadn't done anything except mount little patrols and improve their fortifications.

It was much different from the heady days when they were charging across France and pulverizing the Germans. Crowds cheered them wildly when they liberated towns, but here, in the province of Lorraine, it was a much different situation. Lorraine was on the German border and had been part of Germany until 1919. Many of its citizens were German sympathizers, and some were dedicated Nazis. There had been numerous acts of sabotage and ambush. When the GIs were able to get into a town for a little beer or wine, they had to keep their eyes peeled for snipers. The good old days were over.

But the picture wasn't all bad. Charlie Company had been brought up to full strength, and its ammunition stocks had increased steadily. Everybody said that a new offensive was in the offing. Mahoney didn't look forward to getting shot at again, but sometimes he thought it might be better than sitting around in wet foxholes all the time.

He finished his C ration meal and lit up a cigarette. A

PRESENTING

The *Louis L'Amour* Collection

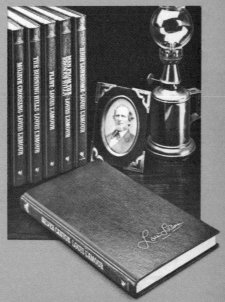

Explore <u>Silver Canyon</u>,
your first handsome hardcover
Collector's Edition
for 10 days <u>FREE</u>

Enjoy the best of Louis L'Amour in special volumes made to last as long as your pleasure

As a reader of Louis L'Amour's tough and gritty tales of the Old West, you'll be delighted by <u>The Louis L'Amour Collection</u>— a series of hardcover editions of Louis L'Amour's exciting Western adventures.

The feel of rich leathers. Like a good saddle, these volumes are made to last—to be read, re-read and passed along to family and friends for years to come. Bound in rugged sierra-brown simulated leather with gold lettering, <u>The Louis L'Amour Collection</u> will be a handsome addition to your home library.

<u>Silver Canyon</u> opens the series. It's the memorable tale of Matt Brennan, gunfighter, and his lone battle against duelling ranchers in one of the bloodiest range wars the West had ever seen. After <u>Silver Canyon</u> you'll set out on a new adventure every month, as succeeding volumes in the Collection are conveniently mailed to your home.

Receive the full-color Louis L'Amour Western Calendar FREE—just for looking at <u>Silver Canyon</u>. Like every volume in <u>The Louis L'Amour Collection</u>, <u>Silver Canyon</u> is yours to examine without risk or obligation. If you're not satisfied, return it within 10 days and owe nothing. The calendar is yours to keep.

Send no money now. Simply complete the coupon opposite to enter your subscription to <u>The Louis L'Amour Collection</u> and receive your free calendar.

The newest volume...

The newest volume I placed on the shelf of my 8000-volume home research library was very special to me—the first copy of _Silver Canyon_ in the hardcover Collector's Edition put together by the folks at Bantam Books.

I'm very proud of this new collection of my books. They're handsome, permanent and what I like best of all, affordable.

I hope you'll take this opportunity to examine the books in the Collection and see their fine quality for yourself. I think you'll be as pleased as I am!

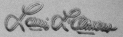

Send no money now—but mail today!

☐ **YES!** Please send me _Silver Canyon_ for a 10-day free examination, along with my free Louis L'Amour Calendar, and enter my subscription to The Louis L'Amour Collection. If I decide to keep _Silver Canyon_, I will pay $7.95 plus shipping and handling and receive one additional volume per month on a fully returnable, 10-day free-examination basis. There is no minimum number of books to buy, and I may cancel my subscription at any time. The Calendar is mine whether or not I keep _Silver Canyon_.   05157

☐ I prefer the deluxe edition, bound in genuine leather, at only $24.95 each plus shipping and handling.   05165

Name   _(please print)_

Address

City   State   Zip

In Canada, mail to:
Bantam Books Canada, Inc.
60 St. Clair Avenue East, Suite 601
Toronto, Ontario M4T 1N5

A 1 2

BUSINESS REPLY MAIL

FIRST CLASS   PERMIT NO. 2154   HICKSVILLE, NY

Postage will be paid by addressee:

The
Louis L'Amour
Collection

Bantam Books
P.O. Box 956
Hicksville, New York 11801

detail from his platoon was digging a new deep trench not far away, and he could hear the shovels clanging against the rocks in the ground. *I should count my blessings,* he thought. *At least I don't have to go out there and dig fucking holes anymore.*

He turtled his head into the poncho so that no rain would drip down his back and puffed his cigarette. In times like this, when he could give his mind free play, he would think about Laura Hubbard and their wild night of love. He recalled the insane positions they'd tried, the incredible blow job she'd given him, and the many times he went down on her. It had been unbelievable; in fact, sometimes he wondered if it had happened at all. The only people who knew what had happened were he and Laura, and he wasn't so sure anymore. He probably never would see her again in his life and never could get verification. Was it all just a wet dream? he wondered. He remembered that an old depraved sergeant had told him once that no woman ever could hope to give a man what he got in a wet dream. Whether it was a wet dream or not, he was convinced that he'd never attain anything like it again in his life. *It's all downhill for me now,* he thought. *You can only have something like that once in a lifetime.*

"How're you doing down there, sergeant!"

Mahoney looked up and saw Captain Anderson. "Okay, sir," he replied, standing up.

Anderson jumped into the foxhole. "That's okay. You can remain seated."

Mahoney dropped to his haunches again, and Captain Anderson did the same.

"How're your men making out with the new fortifications?" Anderson asked.

"Just fine, considering the ground is full of rocks and it's raining like a son of a bitch."

Anderson scrutinized Mahoney's face. "Are you all right, sergeant?"

"Sure I'm all right," Mahoney replied.

"You haven't looked too well lately. Are you sure you're all right?"

"Who can be all right stuck here in the mud for a month?"

"That's about to come to an end," Anderson said in a low voice. "We're being placed on a twenty-four-hour alert as of tomorrow morning. There'll be no more passes, and I want everybody to be ready to move out upon receipt of orders. Tell your men at the evening formation tonight."

Mahoney's face brightened. "Something's up, huh? Do you know what it is?"

"Not exactly," Anderson replied, "but I hear it's something big."

THIRTEEN

"Metz," said General Patton, pointing to a city on his map. "It's the key to the Saar and the Siegfried Line."

General Walker, the commanding officer of Patton's XX Corps, looked at the section of the map that Patton was indicating. Also around the map table were Patton's staff oficers plus the commanders of the Ninety-Fifth Division, the Ninetieth Division, and General Donovan, of the fighting Thirty-third Division Hammerheads.

"For a time," Patton said, "I had thought we could bypass Metz because it's a strong, well-fortified position and I knew it could be got only at a high price, but lately I've come to the conclusion that we cannot leave that city to our rear because its garrison will be free to harass our supply lines, blow up ammo dumps, stage ambushes, and so forth. Therefore, we'll have to take the damn place head-on." He took a deep breath and placed one hand on his hip. "Metz has a rather interesting military history," he said. "Although many wars have passed around it, it has not been taken by assault since the Huns did it in the year 451 A.D. Many have tried since then, and the city has fallen to siege on numerous occasions, the most recent being during the First World War, but we'll be the first army in almost sixteen hundred years to take it by force of arms. I don't know exactly when we'll attack because so much depends on the weather, but I imagine it will be during the early part of November. The order of battle will be as follows: the 90th will go in on the left, the 95th will go in on the right, and the Hammerheads will go right up the middle. Metz is well defended as far as we know and is protected by numerous natural and man-made obstacles. The Germans know how important the city is, and I suspect they're waiting for us to come. It won't be easy, but

I want that city." Patton looked up from the map table and gazed into the eyes of each of them. "I repeat: *I want that city!*"

The Hammerheads were replaced on the line by the 110th Division on October 31 and loaded into trucks. They were transported through the mud and pouring rain to a sector of the line not far from Metz, where they dug in and waited for orders to attack.

German spies in the area reported the movement to *Armeegruppe G* headquarters, as other spies in the Third Army sector reported similar movements. As the reports came in, General Balck realized that a major effort was underway. He called a meeting of his staff officers and local commanders, advising them that the Americans were planning an offensive but expressing optimism that the Americans could be crushed easily. Once again, he repeated to his officers the contention that Patton was inept and his Third Army a joke.

One officer at the meeting didn't think Patton was inept and the Third Army a joke. He was Gen. Heinrich Freiherr von Luttwitz, who had faced the Third Army in the Falaise Pocket where the Second Panzer Division, which he had commanded at the time, had nearly been wiped off the face of the earth. Now, as commander of the XLVII Panzer Corps, he was responsible for the defense of Metz.

Upon returning to his headquarters, he placed Metz in "Condition Red" and had the city regarrisoned with the 559th Volksgrenadier Division and a makeshift unit called Division Number 462, comprised of fanatical soldiers enrolled in officer and NCO training schools.

Also defending Metz were two replacement infantry battalions, one machine-gun company, one engineer battalion, two antiaircraft battalions, one artillery battalion, four companies of Waffen SS signal-school trainees, some Luftwaffe troops, and the local SS detachment, which was ordered to stop tormenting civilians and prepare to defend Metz to the death.

General von Chevallerie, who commanded the garrison of Metz, was relieved of command because it was felt that he wasn't aggressive enough. He was replaced by Gen. Otto von Neubacher, who wore a Hitler moustache and had distinguished himself in numerous battles.

When Neubacher took command of Metz, he was pleased to learn that all the approaches to the city had been heavily mined. The Americans would make easy targets for his artillery as they struggled to get through those minefields and he ordered his artillery to zero in on them. He conducted an extensive inspection of the city, moving troops around and ordering the construction of special strongholds and bunkers.

Like Patton, Neubacher was aware of the history of Metz, that it had not been taken by assault since A.D. 451. One day, while standing on the roof of the tallest building in the city, he studied his fortifications through binoculars and decided that Metz probably wouldn't be taken by assault again for another sixteen hundred years, certainly not for as long as he remained commander of the garrison there.

A patrol from the Twenty-eighth Regiment of the Hammer-head Division wandered into a minefield one night, setting off three Bouncing Betties and killing three of the soldiers. The explosions made trigger-happy Germans think the attack was beginning, and they opened up with everything they had on the section of the minefield where they'd seen the flashes of light.

In the ensuing minutes, hell rained down on that part of the minefield, killing three more of the soldiers. But two managed to escape and report back to their headquarters. That's how the existence of the minefields became known among the American commanders, and a plan was devised so that when the bombardment of Metz was to begin, some of the artillery pieces were to aim at the minefield and blow up as many of the mines as possible.

On the first of November, the offensive was ready to begin but was held in abeyance for clear weather so that air support could be provided. The days passed, and the weather did not improve. Finally, Patton decided to go ahead without air support. He ordered that the attack begin on the morning of November 8 no matter what.

The soldiers prepared for battle and prayed that the rain would stop, but it didn't. On the evening of November 7, Patton was pacing the floor in his headquarters near the front when there was a knock on the door.

"Come in!" he said.

The door opened, and Generals Eddy and Grow entered the room. They were the commanders of the Ninth Infantry and Sixth Armored Divisions, respectively, two old war dogs who'd been in the army for most of their lives.

"Sir," said Eddy, "is the offensive still on?"

Patton looked at him as though he were mad. "Of course it's still on!" he bellowed.

"But, sir," protested Grow, "we can't attack in weather like this!"

"Oh, yes, we can!" Patton retorted.

"The rivers are swollen, and we won't have air support. It'll be a disaster."

Patton looked at both of them angrily. "The attack will go off as scheduled! If you don't want to lead your troops, tell me now and I'll relieve you of command!"

"Sir," said Eddy, "we urge you to reconsider. Weather like this can stop an attack worse than enemy resistance."

"I'll say it once more, and that will be all!" Patton replied. "The attack will go off as scheduled! Are you gentlemen in or out!"

Eddy and Grow looked at each other and realized that they couldn't change Patton's mind.

"I'm in," said Eddy.

"Me, too," added Grow.

"Then get the hell back where you belong!" Patton told them.

In Charlie Company, Mahoney sat in a foxhole filled with mud and water, shivering and smoking a cigarette. He couldn't sleep as always before a big attack, and neither could Cranepool, who was in the foxhole with him. They looked up at the sky and could see a few stars through the clouds, but it still was raining, anyway, although not as heavily as earlier.

They didn't speak because they had nothing to talk about. The details of the attack had been hashed over a hundred times, and they both knew what to do. The artillery preparation would begin at five o'clock in the morning and would destroy, among other things, the minefield directly in front of them. Then they'd cross the minefield and approach the section of the Moselle River directly in front of Metz. They'd cross the river in boats, and on the other side they'd land directly in the city. Then they'd begin to capture it building by building. Everything would be easier if they had air support, but they didn't, so they'd have to do the best they could.

When 0500 hours came, the artillery bombardment didn't begin.

"Maybe the attack's been called off," Cranepool said.

"Maybe," Mahoney replied.

They puffed their cigarettes and wondered what had happened.

FOURTEEN

The artillery bombardment began at 0515 hours, slightly behind schedule. The sound of the guns woke up General Patton, who'd been sleeping with his clothes on. He put on his poncho and helmet and went outside.

It was still raining, though much less than before. In the distance, he could see the horizon ablaze with explosions from left to right. The ground shook as if an earthquake were taking place.

Those poor goddamned Germans, Patton thought.

"Charge!" screamed Captain Anderson, pumping his right hand up and down in the air, the signal for double time.

Charlie Company followed him out of the woods and into the field. To their left and right were other companies in the battalion, and they all were formed into three long skirmish lines. Behind them were trucks filled with engineers and boats for crossing the river. Ahead of them were noisy, clanking tanks.

The men ran across the minefield, jumping over shell craters and shouting battle cries. German observers in the towers of Metz saw them coming and ordered the artillery batteries still in action to open fire.

German shells fell on the field, and German machine guns raked it back and forth, but the GIs kept driving.

Mahoney held his carbine near his stomach and ran with his head low like a fullback on a football team about to smash through the other team's line. Some of the Bouncing Betties hadn't been detonated by the bombardment, and a few of them blew soldiers in half, but the others kept running for the back of the river. Some of them thought it strange that they'd crossed the same river a month ago, but the Moselle took many extreme twists and turns, and although the American lines were far ahead of certain portions of it, they were behind it near Metz.

The tanks fired their cannons as they rolled noisily across the field, filling the air with bitter diesel fumes. One of the tanks in front of Charlie Company was knocked on to its side by an antitank mine, but the next tank passed it and roared forward, firing its cannon.

The artillery bombardment of Metz continued, and the city was hidden in sheets of flame. Mahoney figured he'd be safer once he got over the river and into those buildings, but safety was a relative thing because he knew the city would be crawling with Germans. He looked to his right and left and saw some of his new men losing their positions in the line.

"Dress right and wake the fuck up!" he shouted. "Let's go!"

The tanks reached the banks of the Moselle, stopped, and fired at the buildings on the other side. The soldiers took positions behind the tanks and fired their weapons, although they couldn't see anything except fire and the vague outlines of buildings.

The trucks rolled through the openings and stopped at the river bank. Engineers unloaded the boats and crates of life jackets. An engineer officer blew a whistle three times, the signal to load on to the boats. The soldiers ran down to the river bank and lined up in their respective places as the tanks fired cannons and .50 caliber machine guns over their heads.

Mahoney grabbed a life jacket and put it on. *"Move your fucking asses!"* he screamed, pushing and kicking them. *"Get into that goddamn boat!"*

His new replacements were frightened and confused, and he knew the only thing to do was make them more afraid of him than the Germans straight ahead. One replacement, Private Rubaldino of Oakland, California, panicked and started to run back in the direction from which they'd come.

Mahoney took two huge leaps and grabbed Rubaldino by the collar of his field jacket. *"Where the fuck do you think you're going!"*

Rubaldino looked at Mahoney with terror in his eyes. Mahoney dragged him back to the boat and pushed him inside. Mahoney looked from side to side and saw men loading into boats, some of them moving out into the fast-moving river already.

"Let's go!" he yelled. "Move it out!"

Artillery shells fell on the city of Metz, and the din was terrific. The explosions and fires flickered against the faces of the GIs as they jumped into the boats. Once again, Mahoney chose Cranepool's first squad to cross with. He sat in the stern of the boat, and the engineers pushed them off. A big replacement named Jones pulled one of the oars, and Cranepool pulled the other. Mahoney looked ahead at Metz and wondered if it would become his tomb.

The boats moved into the river, and German fire was light because the artillery bombardment made it difficult for them to fire. Jones and Cranepool rowed as quickly as they could because they wanted to get as close to the city as possible before the artillery stopped.

Gradually, the American artillery "walked" in from the shoreline so no short shells would fall on the Americans. The Germans in the forward buildings took positions in windows and on roofs, firing down at the boats, but there weren't many Germans left and their fire was light.

"Row!" Mahoney screamed, gritting his teeth. "Let's get the fuck over there!"

The river moved swiftly, but Cranepool and Jones were able to keep in a fairly straight line. A few bullets whistled over their heads, but it was nothing compared to their previous Moselle crossings. Behind them, engineers were already at work on the pontoon bridges that would permit the tanks to cross the river. The tanks were still firing their cannons and machine guns at the Germans, preventing them from aiming accurately.

The air was filled with smoke and shouts. Mahoney peered ahead and saw a wall made of boulders extending six feet above the surface of the water. He and his men would have to jump out of their boats and go over the wall to get into Metz. That didn't look as if it would be an easy job.

Private Rubaldino was whimpering and blubbering in the hold of the boat. His eyes darted about like a cornered rat, and Mahoney thought he might jump overboard. Mahoney reached forward and grabbed Rubaldino by the front of his field jacket.

"You'd better shape the fuck up, young soldier!" Mahoney snarled.

Rubaldino whined, and Mahoney hauled off and punched him in the mouth. Rubaldino's lip split open and two teeth were knocked loose from their roots. He looked at Mahoney with bulging eyes, bracing himself for another punch.

"I said you'd better shape up!" Mahoney repeated.

Rubaldino wiped the blood from his mouth and tried to stop blubbering, but he was only half successful. Mahoney looked forward and saw the stone wall coming closer. He spotted some wooden pilings and metal fittings evidently used by townspeople to tie up their boats in happier days.

"Trask!" shouted Mahoney. "Do you see those things on the wall?"

Trask, who was sitting in the bow of the boat, looked straight ahead. "What things on the wall!"

"Those wooden things!"

"Yeah, I see them!"

"Grab one when we get close!"

"Hup, sarge!"

Cranepool and Jones strained against their oars, and the boat moved closer to the wall. Mahoney looked to his right and left and saw the other boats slowly making their way across the river. Some of them had already reached the wall, and the men were climbing up the boulders to the river-front boulevard above them. Mahoney hoped the tanks would come across quickly. It might get a little hot up there without tanks to provide cover.

The boat banged against the wall, and Trask grabbed an eye hook protruding from a column of rotting wood.

"Up the fucking wall!" Mahoney yelled. "Let's hit it!"

Cranepool dropped his oars, turned around, and leaped toward the boulders, digging in his hands and feet and scrambling up like a jackrabbit. The other men followed him, some slower and some faster. Rubaldino cowered in the boat and looked up pleadingly at Mahoney.

"I can't move!" he wailed.

Mahoney aimed his carbine down and pulled the trigger. The floorboards exploded next to Rubaldino's feet, and Rubaldino jumped two feet into the air. When he came down, he saw water burbling through the jagged hole in the hull.

"You can stay if you want to," Mahoney said, stepping over him. "I don't give a fuck."

"Wait for me!" Rubaldino yelled, stumbling toward the boulders.

Mahoney began to climb up. "Let's go!" he said to Trask. "You can come up now!"

Trask took hold of a boulder and began to climb. Rubaldino, his hands trembling and tears pouring down his cheeks, tried to fasten himself to the wall, but he was shaking too much, and the boat was bobbing up and down. Without Trask to hold it to the wall, it began drifting away.

"Wait for me!" Rubaldino shrieked.

"Wait for you, my ass!" Mahoney replied, climbing up the wall.

Rubaldino realized he had to take action quickly or go down with the boat. He leaped toward the wall, but the boat zipped away underneath him, and he fell into the roaring Moselle. He splashed his hands wildly, trying to reach the wall, but the river dragged him downstream.

"Help!" he screamed. "Help!"

"Help your ass," Mahoney grumbled as he climbed the wall. His head cleared the top of it, and he saw the wide boulevard and the buildings on the other side. His men were running across the boulevard as Germans fired down at them from the windows and roofs of the buildings.

Mahoney vaulted over the wall and ran across the boulevard, holding his carbine in his right hand. Bullets slammed into the asphalt near him, but he kept pumping his legs, seeing his platoon huddled against the wall of a building.

"Don't bunch up!" he yelled. "Get the fuck inside!"

The men rushed toward the downstairs door. Cranepool was first, firing his carbine at the lock. The door shattered, and he pushed it open.

"Hurry up—get inside!" Mahoney screamed.

Something slammed against Mahoney's helmet and bounced off. It was a German hand grenade, and as it passed his eyes, he thought he was a goner for sure. He tried to catch it so he could throw it away, but he bobbled it, and it dropped toward the ground. When it was level with his knees, he thought, *Oh, my God, it's going to blow my dick off,* but as it fell lower, he kicked it through a basement window of the building and dived through the first floor door.

The grenade exploded, blasting the frame off the basement window, and Mahoney thanked God that it didn't blow his dick off. Ahead of him, Cranepool and the others were firing rifles and killing Germans, trying to rush them through doors. The room filled with gunsmoke, and soldiers screamed as they toppled to the floor, leaking blood. Mahoney pulled one of his grenades out of a pocket and yanked the pin, hurling it through one of the doors. The house shook with the explosion, and chunks of wood flew in all directions, but no more Germans came through that door. His men followed his example, throwing grenades through the other doors, and the building shook so violently that Mahoney thought it might cave in on their heads.

They coughed in the smoke and dust, firing their rifles and carbines, but they heard no more Germans. Mahoney realized they had one room secured, and at least that was a start. He looked around and saw the room filled with his men. There were too many of them in one place. One German hand grenade could wipe out his whole platoon.

"I'm gonna split up the platoon," he said. "Squads one and two will try to take this building, and squads three and four will take the one next door. Cranepool will be in overall charge of this building, and I'll take squads three and four next door. Any questions?"

Nobody said anything.

"Let's hit it!"

Mahoney hurtled through the door, and the third and fourth squads followed him outside. He saw hordes of American soldiers crossing the boulevard and attacking buildings. The Germans threw hand grenades off the roofs and out the windows, blowing up GIs, but the GIs moved grimly into the city, holding their heads down and looking for cover.

Mahoney and his two squads dashed toward the building next door.

"Throw hand grenades through all the windows!" he told them.

They took out grenades, pulled pins, and hurled them through all the windows on the first floor and basement. Then they dropped to the sidewalk as the building seemed to dance up and down with the ferocious explosions. As soon as the last one went off, Mahoney was up and swooping toward the front door, firing his carbine on automatic. The door shattered before the .30-caliber bullets, and he kicked it open, still firing as he charged into the room.

A German showed his face in a doorway, and Mahoney directed a stream of bullets at it, reducing the head to a bloody, pulpy mass. The German didn't have time to make a sound; he just toppled to the floor. Mahoney heard another sound and turned in its direction. Another German appeared in a doorway but before Mahoney could get set, Butsko drilled the German through his lower abdomen. Two Germans charged through another doorway, and Pvt. Jethro Doakes of Rinnie, Tennessee, cut them down with his BAR, the first men he'd ever killed in his life.

A flight of stairs led down into the room they were in, and three Germans descended it, firing submachine guns. They killed two of Mahoney's men and wounded three others before they were shot, and they tumbled down the stairs, leaving a trail of blood behind them.

"Medic!" Mahoney yelled through one of the windows. "I wanna medic in here!"

Out on the street, a tall, skinny medic with a nose like a banana spun around at the sound of Mahoney's voice and ran toward the building holding his steel pot steady on his head. He ran up the steps, entered the room, and saw the wounded GIs on the floor. Kneeling, he went to work, taking bandages and sulfa out of his haversack.

Mahoney slung his carbine crossways over his shoulder and chest and picked up one of the German submachine guns.

"Let's take the next floor!" he said.

The men followed him up the stairs to the next landing. A German poked his head through a door, and Mahoney shot it off with the submachine gun. Two more Germans appeared in another doorway, but a hail of bullets fired by five GI's all at once sent them flying backward, spurting blood in all directions.

Mahoney and his men charged on to the second-floor landing, tossing hand grenades into the rooms and then firing bullets. They rushed into the rooms, cutting down Germans still alive or wounded, and then, out on the landing, were horrified to see three hand grenades come bouncing down the stairs.

"Get back!" Mahoney screamed.

They dived into the rooms, and the grenades exploded in the landing outside, ripping apart plaster and cracking timbers that had been there for a hundred years. A tornado of dust and smoke swept into all the rooms, and the soldiers coughed, their eyes burning.

Mahoney wiped his nose with the back of his hand and wondered what to do. Those hand grenades were getting to be a problem, and all the Germans had to do was lob them down the stairwell. Somehow he and his men had to go up on one roof, and then they could start coming down on the Germans and having all the advantages themselves.

"Hey, sarge," said Butsko, "you all right?"

"Yeah, I'm all right."

"I thought you were sleeping over there."

Mahoney looked sideways at Butsko and thought seriously for the first time about killing him; he was getting to be a terrific pain in the ass.

"Our only chance," Mahoney told the men around him, "is to get up on the roof of this building as quickly as we can. We'll go up in waves of two, with five seconds between each wave. One man in each wave will go up with his weapon ready to fire at anything that moves, and the other man will go up ready to scoop up and dispose of any hand grenade that comes his way. Any questions?"

Pvt. Teddy Dubois of Bangor, Maine, raised his hand. "Dispose of them how?" he asked.

"Just throw the fucking things away."

"Where?"

"Wherever we aren't, you stupid cocksucker. Are we ready?"

They didn't look ready, but nobody dared to say anything. Mahoney lined them up in ranks of twos, he and Private Doakes going up first and Butsko and an old veteran named Lewis second. He designated which ones would fire their weapons and which would deal with hand grenades. He told them that in the first rank he and Doakes would both fire their automatic weapons to clear the way and that the people behind them had better keep their eyes open for grenades.

"All right," he said, "when I give the word, we move out and go like hell. Speed is everything. Everybody ready?"

He looked them over sternly, and no one had the temerity to say anything. Some looked frightened, the rest angry and determined. Mahoney got in front with Doakes, who had fed a fresh clip into his BAR.

"Go!" yelled Mahoney.

He and Doakes charged on to the landing and ran toward the stairs, which were splintered and shaky due to the hand-grenade explosions. They bounded up the stairs three at a time, holding their weapons ready, and saw grenades falling like apples toward them.

"Get those grenades!" Mahoney screamed.

The men behind him scrambled for the grenades and threw them into empty rooms or down the stairwell. Mahoney and Doakes reached the second floor and sprayed the doorways on the landing even though they saw no Germans. They turned the corner and started up the next flight of stairs as more grenades fell toward them.

"Here come some more!" Mahoney yelled.

He heard footsteps above and knew that Germans were coming down to fight. The GIs behind him snatched hand grenades out of the air and threw them away. The stairwell rocked with the explosions, and Mahoney saw German uniforms on the third landing. He and Doakes opened fire at the same moment, and so did the Germans. A German bullet sliced through Doakes's left lung, and he fell back, knocking over the soldier behind him.

Mahoney rushed the third-floor landing all alone, firing the submachine gun from side to side and gritting his teeth. Germans were crowded together on the landing, bumping into each other as they tried to get set and return the fire, but they had been cooks and file clerks a few weeks before and didn't have a chance. Mahoney's bullets cut them down, and the ones in back panicked, trying to run away. They tried to flee up the stairs, and Mahoney went after them spraying their backs with bullets. The Germans tripped and stumbled, pirouetting in the air and falling backward. Mahoney got out of the way, and the Germans fell past him to the landing below.

"Keep moving!" Mahoney yelled. "Follow me!"

He leaped up the stairs three at a time, firing the submachine gun, but no more Germans appeared above him. On the fourth landing, he fed a fresh clip into the submachine gun.

"Let's go!" he shouted. "Hurry up!"

He climbed the stairs to the fifth landing, looking for the movement of field-gray German uniforms, and saw a sleeve in a doorway. He fired a burst at the sleeve, but it darted out of the way.

"The last two men get the kraut in that room!" Mahoney screamed, running past the doorway on the way up to the roof.

The door to the roof opened, and a hand grenade came flying down at him. He dodged out of the way and kept charging.

"Get that grenade!"

He reached the top step and dove head first through the doorway, landing on the pebbles on the roof as the hand grenade blew off somewhere behind him. Machine-gun bullets zapped beside him, and he rolled out of the way, looking for cover. Germans fired at him from behind skylights and chimneys, and the third and fourth squads exploded through the doorway and charged on to the roof, firing as they came searching for cover. German machine guns cut down a few of them, and the rest yanked out hand grenades, dropping to their bellies.

A bullet smashed into the roof two inches from Mahoney's head as he yanked a grenade from his lapel. He pulled the pin and hurled it toward a machine-gun nest he could see in a corner of the roof, and it was a perfect throw, the grenade landing in the midst of the Germans. They looked at it in total horror, frozen with the realization of what was about to happen to them, and then the grenade blasted them into the air, and one of them was thrown over the parapet.

That eliminated some of the hostile fire on the roof. His men fired desperately at the other Germans on the roof, who were hiding everywhere, and one of the Germans tried to throw a hand grenade of his own, but he was shot through the head just as his hand went back, and he fell among his comrades, the hand grenade exploding and ripping them apart.

Mahoney issued orders that sent his men attacking the remaining Germans in waves. The GIs advanced a few feet at a time, slowly closing in on the Germans, who were being pinned down by fire from other GIs. One German managed to throw a hand grenade that blew up two men in the fourth squad, but within fifteen minutes, all the Germans on that roof were overcome.

The Americans couldn't stand up and look around because Germans on the next roof were firing at them. Mahoney crouched behind the parapet and lit a cigarette, formulating a way to attack the next building.

FIFTEEN

Throughout the early hours of the morning, Patton and his generals stood at the map table as reports trickled in on the progress of his offensive. They moved pins around and were pleased with the amount of ground that had been taken. All units up and down the Third Army line had reached their assigned objectives and were pushing forward steadily. Now that they had gas and ammunition, it was like the old days except that the Germans had used the month of October to reorganize and were offering stiff resistance everywhere. Patton thought his casualties were heavier than they should have been, thanks to Ike and the jokers at Supreme Headquarters Allied Expeditionary Forces (SHAEF).

At eight o'clock, a call came in from Gen. Omar Bradley at EAGLE TAC, and the phone was handed to Patton.

"What are your plans for today, George?" Bradley asked.

"I'm attacking," Patton replied. "Can't you hear my guns?"

"What!" Bradley replied. "You're attacking without air support?"

"That's right."

There was a pause for a few moments. "I don't know if that was a good idea, George."

"We're doing okay."

"You are?"

"We've reached all our designated objectives so far."

"What about Metz?"

"My Hammerhead Division is fighting inside the city limits."

"Why that's splendid, George!" Bradley said, his voice becoming enthusiastic. "I wouldn't have thought it possible without air support!"

"The weather is hurting the Germans as much as it's hurting us."

"Hang on a moment, will you?"

"Yes, sir."

Patton stood with a phone next to his ear, looking down at the map table. Even he was surprised at the progress his troops were making without air cover, but he saw no point in admitting it.

"George?" asked Bradley.

"I'm here," Patton replied.

"Ike is here, George, and he wants to speak with you."

"Ike!"

"That's right. Here he is."

Patton waited and a few seconds later heard the velvety voice of Gen. Dwight D. Eisenhower.

"George, this is Ike, your supreme commander!" he said. "I'm thrilled by your offensive, boy! I expect a hell of a lot from you, so carry the ball all the way!"

"Thanks, general," Patton said with a faint smile. "We'll carry it, sir—we sure will!"

"I hear you're doing real well, George!"

"As well as can be expected, sir, all things considered."

"That's fine. You just keep on doing what you're doing. And give your men my best regards. Tell them I expect a lot from them in this campaign."

"Yes, sir."

Patton hung up the phone, his face expressing cynicism. Ike had held him back over a month, giving the Germans an opportunity to regroup opposite the Third Army, and now Ike wanted to give everybody his regards. Sometimes Patton thought that Ike wasn't tied together very tightly.

"Everything all right, sir?" asked General Maddox.

"Nobody's telling us to stop," Patton replied, returning to the map table, "so I suppose everything's okay. Has anything happened while I was on the phone? Where are we now?"

"My *Fuehrer*," said General Jodl, "I'm afraid I have more bad news."

Hitler looked up from his desk and the documents strewn upon it. Although it was morning in East Prussia, all the curtains in his office were drawn because sunlight hurt his eyes. "What is it now?"

"General Patton has launched an all-out offensive in Lorraine," Jodl said, standing at ease in front of Hitler's desk. "General Balck requests reinforcements urgently."

Hitler shook his head. "Absolutely not!"

"He says that he is faced with superior numbers of troops and tanks and that he must retreat."

"Jodl," said Hitler sternly, "you will tell Balck that he must hold Alsace-Lorraine regardless of the circumstances. He must fight for time. On no account should he allow a situation to develop in which my forces earmarked for the Ardennes offensive would have to be sidetracked to his army group. Make that clear to him. Do you understand?"

"But, my *Fuehrer*," Jodl said, "there often comes a time in battles where an army must retreat or lose everything."

Hitler rose unsteadily to his feet, his face drained of color. Lightning bolts of rage shot out of his hypnotic eyes, and Jodl regretted having raised that objection to his *Fuehrer*.

"My good Jodl," Hitler said in his deep, hoarse voice, "our most severe losses seem to come from our 'glorious' retreats, the ones we make so that we don't lose everything. But when we stand and fight, quite often we win victories that no one except me thinks we can win."

Jodl could have mentioned instances where the German army stood and fought and got wiped out, such as in North Africa under Rommel, but he decided to be prudent this time. "Yes, my *Fuehrer*," he said softly.

"Furthermore," Hitler added, "even if the enemy offensive in Alsace-Lorraine should create major inroads into our territory and fortifications, we must accept that risk for the sake of my Ardennes buildup. Do I make myself clear?"

"Yes, my *Fuehrer*."

"Transmit my wishes to General Balck."

"Yes, my *Fuehrer*."

Jodl turned around and walked out of Hitler's office, wondering exactly what he should tell Balck, for on the one hand Hitler ordered that Balck stand fast, and then he also said it was all right to retreat. *I'm sure I'll think of something suitably equivocal by the time I get to the communications office*, he thought. *I always do.*

SIXTEEN

At Metz, by ten o'clock in the morning, the rain had stopped, the sun came out, and American planes attacked the forts that ringed the city plus German strongholds within the city itself. Mahoney and his third and fourth squads stood on the roof of a building and watched the planes swoop out of the sky, dropping bombs and strafing targets. The sky became crisscrossed with vapor trails as the planes dived and climbed into the sky again.

Mahoney removed his canteen out of its case and took a swig. He had his two machine-gun sections set up on the roof, and thus far his platoon had cleared out four houses. From the streets below he could hear the sounds of American Sherman tanks dueling German Tigers and Panthers. American howitzers had been moved forward and set up, and their shells were reducing stubborn pockets of resistance to piles of rubble. The GIs were ripping into Metz systematically, but they still had a long way to go before they could say the city was theirs.

"Okay, fuckheads," Mahoney said, "let's get the next building."

He put his canteen into his case and snapped the case shut. Then, his submachine gun in his right hand, he ran and jumped over the alley, landing on the roof of the next building. As his feet slammed down, he knew he could be heard throughout the building, and any Germans there would get ready for a fight, but at least there weren't any of them on the roof. The American planes had driven them into the buildings, and it wouldn't be easy to get them out.

The rest of the men jumped the alley and advanced behind him toward the door that led down into the building. A face appeared in the doorway and ducked back. Butsko had been ready for that and hurled a hand grenade into the doorway. He and his men dropped on their stomachs, and the hand grenade exploded, ripping out the walls of the little roof house. An American plane zoomed past just over their heads as they rushed the doorway, and Mahoney was first inside.

He saw a German soldier plastered all over one of the shattered walls. Mahoney ran past him toward the stairs, aiming his submachine gun down, when the bullet whistled past his ear. He dodged backward, jumping into his men.

"Don't follow me so close!" he yelled, pulling out his hand grenade, his next to last. He yanked the pin and tossed the grenade to the landing below, then kneeled so the shrapnel wouldn't take his head off by mistake.

The grenade exploded, sending billows of smoke up the stairs, and Mahoney jumped over the bannister, landing on the next flight of stairs, only a few steps from the landing. He hopped down the three stairs, firing his submachine gun as he went, and when he reached the landing, he spun around like a madman, firing into all the doorways, as his men followed him and spread out to take the rooms one by one.

During the course of the fighting that morning, Mahoney had worked out a plan of attack for taking houses, and now he didn't have to give orders anymore; they just went from building to building doing the same thing. When they had one floor cleared, they took the floor below it, and so forth. After they'd killed every German in the building, they went up to the roof again and jumped to the next building, where they'd do it all over again.

Slowly, they made their way into the building. Mahoney threw his last grenade on the fourth floor and had to borrow some from men who hadn't thrown many of them. He'd had ten men killed so far and four wounded seriously enough to be evacuated.

On the first floor, Mahoney kicked open a door and charged into a butcher shop. German soldiers hid behind meat cases and chopping blocks, firing at the Americans, who fanned out as they entered the room, overwhelming the remaining Germans, but the Germans managed to kill two more of Mahoney's men, and when the smoke had cleared, he only had ten left, including himself.

"Butsko," he said, "take two men and see if anybody's

down in the basement. Hamm, see if you can find any steaks in the cooler.''

The three men left the group to carry out their orders, and Mahoney took off his helmet, wiping his forehead with the back of his arm. He looked at Riggs, who was standing nearby like a puppy dog, waiting for an order to do something.

''Gimme the walkie-talkie.''

''Hup, sarge.''

Mahoney took the walkie-talkie and tromped toward the front door of the butcher shop. He unlatched the door and opened it, hearing an increase in the sounds of battle. Stepping on to the sidewalk, he looked right and left and saw troops running down the street. An American tank was set up at an intersection, and its machine guns were firing at something while its big cannon was elevated in the air.

Mahoney stepped into the street as far as he dared, raised the walkie-talkie to his face, and said: ''Lightning One calling King Lightning—over.'' He let the button go and heard only static and scrambled voices. Pressing the button again, he spoke the code words and still couldn't reach Captain Anderson. After trying two more times, he realized that the tall buildings made radio communication impossible. He'd have to send a runner and thought Riggs might get lost or fall into the hands of the Germans. Someone else would have to go.

He returned to the shop, and Private Hamm was there with the rest of them.

''No steaks, sarge,'' he said. ''Not even no bones.''

Mahoney took out a cigarette and lit it up. He sat down on the floor and took off his helmet. ''Take ten,'' he said.

Butsko returned from the basement. ''Nobody downstairs, Mahoney.''

''Any booze?''

''If there was, I'd have it with me.''

''If there was, you'd probably stash it away someplace so you could come back later and have it all for yourself, you little fuck.''

Butsko grinned. ''Who me, sarge? I always take care of my buddies because they take care of me.''

"I want you to do something for me, Butsko," Mahoney said. "I want you to find Captain Anderson and tell him that we need ammo, grenades, and all the usual shit. Got the picture."

"Hup, sarge."

"You think you can find him?"

"He's gotta be around here someplace. I'll find him."

"Take with you whoever you want and get going."

"Hup, sarge."

Butsko picked his buddy Kubiak, who was from Duquesne, Pennsylvania, which wasn't far from Butsko's home town of McKeesport. They left the shop through the front door and turned left. Mahoney puffed his cigarette and had a drink from his canteen.

"I changed my mind," Mahoney said. "We're gonna stay here until Butsko gets back, so we might as well have chow."

He took off his pack, removed a can of C rations, and looked at the words stenciled on the side: sausage patties.

"Anybody want to trade beans or macaroni for some nice sausage patties?" he asked.

Nobody replied, and they all looked away from Mahoney.

Shit, he thought, taking out his tiny can opener and cutting into the lid. *I wonder if these things really are made out of dog food like everybody says*.

Two blocks away, Butsko and Kubiak saw Private, First Class Drago leaning out a first-floor window and holding his radio aerial high in the air.

"What're you doing," Butsko asked, "goosing butterflies?"

"Captain Anderson is trying to raise the platoon leaders."

"Where the fuck is he?"

"In here."

Butsko and Kubiak climbed the stoop and entered the hallway of the building. They came to a doorway and went inside, seeing Captain Anderson and Sergeant Tweed sitting in a sumptuous living room that had bullet holes in the walls and bloodstains on the rug.

Captain Anderson appeared surprised to see them. "Where are you two coming from?" he asked.

"Down the street," Butsko said. "Sergeant Mahoney sent us here to ask about getting more ammo, hand grenades, and further orders."

"Where is he?"

Butsko pointed. "Thataway."

Anderson leaned forward on the maroon sofa he'd been sitting on and looked at the street map he'd laid on the coffee table. "C'mere, Butsko," he said.

Butsko sauntered over.

Anderson pointed to the map. "If you and I are here right now, where is Mahoney in relation to us?"

Butsko placed his filthy fingernail on the map. "Around here."

"What's your situation?"

Butsko explained that Mahoney had split up the platoon, and he didn't know what had happened to the first and second squads, but the third and fourth had lost about a dozen men.

"Tell Mahoney," Anderson said, "to link up with his first two squads and move in this direction." He pointed to the map. "Understand?"

"Yes, sir."

Anderson didn't believe him. "I'll write it all down. Meanwhile, you and Kubiak go next door and see the supply sergeant about getting some ammo and grenades for now."

"Yes, sir."

Butsko and Kubiak walked back to the kitchen, while Captain Anderson wrote his message on a sheet of paper.

A half hour later, Butsko and Kubiak were on their way back to Mahoney and the third and fourth squads. They were festooned with bandoliers of ammunition, and each carried the handle of a crate of hand grenades. They smoked cigarettes and felt the mild sense of freedom a soldier enjoys when he's on his own and away from his commanding officers and sergeants.

They were taking a short cut and walking down a street that had been the scene of bitter fighting earlier in the day. Walls of the houses were pitted by rifle fire and fragmentation explosions, windows were blown out, huge craters were in the street, and some building façades had been blasted away completely.

They smoked cigarettes and chatted about their former happy lives in Pennsylvania. Halfway down the block, Butsko looked up at the window of a building and was astonished to see the face of a beautiful blonde girl. He stopped in his tracks and ogled her. She smiled and stepped back from the window.

"Did you see that!" Butsko said.

"See what?" Kubiak replied.

"The babe."

"What babe?"

Butsko pointed. "The one in the window there."

"I don't see no babe in the window there."

"She was there just a minute ago!"

"You're out of your fucking mind."

"She was!"

"You shit, too, if you eat regular."

"She smiled at me!"

"Sure she did."

"Well," Butsko said, "I don't give a fuck what you say. I'm going in there. You can wait here if you want to, or you can come in, too."

"But Sergeant Mahoney's waiting for us."

"Fuck him. Let him wait a little while longer."

Kubiak wrinkled his nose. "I don't know, Butsko. This doesn't sound right to me."

"Just wait for me in the hallway up there. I won't be long."

"What're you gonna do?"

Butsko winked. "I'm gonna fuck her."

"Just like that?"

"Sure."

"You're crazy."

"Wait for me in the hall, okay? I won't be any longer than fifteen minutes."

'I don't know." Kubiak didn't want to get into trouble with Mahoney, but he didn't want Butsko to think he was chicken-shit, either. "Oh, what the fuck—okay."

"Maybe I can talk her into giving you a little, too." Butsko winked lasciviously.

"Yeah, sure."

They carried the crate of hand grenades up the steps of the

building and into the hallway. Kubiak sat on the crate and lit another cigarette while Butsko stomped off in the direction of the room where he'd seen the girl.

Butsko opened doors and passed through hallways, looking for the blonde. The rooms reminded him of the one Captain Anderson had been in, with expensive furniture and lots of space. Rich people must have lived here, Butsko thought. That blonde probably is one of those fancy bitches.

He turned a corner and saw her down the end of a hall. She leaned seductively against the opening of a door, a faint smile on her face. Butsko couldn't believe his good fortune. *She wants to get fucked*, he thought happily

"Hi," he said, quickening his pace.

She winked and disappeared into the doorway.

He went after her like a big husky bear. At the doorway, he saw a flight of stairs leading to a cellar. It looked dark and gloomy down there, but he didn't hesitate a moment. He hopped down the stairs, the bandoliers of ammunition jangling around his neck. The blonde had looked beautiful and sexy. Butsko was excited as he peered through the darkness and tried to find her.

"Where are you?" he asked.

She replied in German and didn't sound far away.

Butsko went crashing through the cellar, pushing aside a baby carriage and an old wooden chair. The cellar smelled damp and musty and was cluttered with old furniture.

He entered a room and saw her standing beside a cot, unbuttoning her blouse. Her head was cocked to the side, and she wore a seductive smile. Butsko stared at her for a moment, then leaned his rifle against the wall.

"Hi," he said with a big smile.

He took off his helmet, showing his thick blond hair. His face looked greedy, like a fat wolf about to enjoy a meal. Unbuttoning his shirt, he stepped toward the blonde.

Suddenly, the room filled with thunder as lights flashed from a door on the other side of the room. Butsko felt bullets slicing into him, and cried out as he dropped to the floor. He pressed his hands against the gashes in his body and howled in pain as SS men in black uniforms entered the room through the door and stood around him.

One of them said something in German and chuckled as he bent over and aimed his pistol at Butsko's head. He pulled the trigger, and Butsko's head shattered like a rotten watermelon.

Lieutenant Shroder looked up at the girl and smiled. "Good work," he said.

She nodded, pleased to receive his approval. Five other SS men were in the room.

"He had someone with him," said the girl, whose name was Heidi. "Should I get him, too?"

Shroder nodded his head. Heidi buttoned her blouse and moved toward the doorway. She was tall and slender, with thin lips and an upturned nose. She left the cellar room, and the SS soldiers carried away the bleeding corpse of Ambrose P. Butsko.

Kubiak had been sitting on the box of hand grenades; he jumped to his feet when he heard the volley of gunfire. He grabbed his rifle and pointed it in the direction of the gunfire, wondering what was going on. The gunfire was far enough away so that he knew he was in no great danger; on the other hand, it was close enough to give him cause for concern.

He realized that Butsko was somewhere in that direction. Had he run into some Germans?

Kubiak tiptoed toward the door through which Butsko had passed. "Butsko!" he called out. There was no answer. "Butsko!" Still no answer. Kubiak didn't know what to do. If he waited around, he might find himself in the middle of a war, but he didn't want to leave Butsko. He tried once more. "Butsko!" But still there was no response.

Kubiak decided the best thing to do would be to go back to Mahoney and let him decide what to do; after all, that had been real gunfire he'd heard. He decided to leave the crate of hand grenades behind because he couldn't carry it himself.

He slung his rifle over his shoulder and was about to leave when the blonde appeared in a doorway, smiling at him.

He was relieved to see her. "Where's my friend?" he asked.

She motioned to him with her finger. "*Kommen*," she said with a lewd smile.

"Where's Butsko?"

She ran her tongue over her upper lip, rolled her eyes, and moved back. Kubiak looked at her long, slim body, and his rational thought processes broke down. She turned and walked away, and Kubiak caught a glimpse of her rear end, which he thought had a nice shape to it. Had Butsko sent her up here to get him? Was Butsko lying sated on a bed someplace, smoking a cigarette.

Kubiak went after her. He entered a large room and saw her pass through a door at the other end. He'd always been attracted to slim girls like her. The closer the bone, the sweeter the meat. He continued to pursue her through the opulent rooms of the apartment, and finally she descended the flight of stairs to the cellar.

"Where the hell are you going?" Kubiak asked.

He followed her down the stairs and through the shadows of the cellar rooms. She came to the room with the cot and stood beside it, unbuttoning her blouse.

"Where's Butsko?" Kubiak asked.

She winked and crooked her finger toward him.

Kubiak hadn't been laid in months and couldn't resist this lissome beauty. He moved toward her and wrapped his arms around her waist. She raised her face, and he kissed her lips, thrilled by the taste of young woman, a taste like sour candy.

He heard steps behind him. Pulling his tongue out of her mouth, he was about to turn around when suddenly he felt a shaft of steel enter his back between his shoulder blades. He shrieked with pain, and the blonde girl jumped back. Kubiak staggered, the pain almost unbearably fierce, and coughed blood. The dagger was pulled from his back, and he turned around to see the SS soldiers. "Oh, my God," he mumbled as blood dribbled out of his nose. The German with the dagger in his hand raised his arm and brought it swiftly down. Kubiak tried to raise his hands and fend it off, but he had no strength left. The dagger plunged into his heart, and Kubiak felt a split second of horrible pain. Then the pain and everything else went away as he dropped lifeless to the floor of the cellar.

The Germans looked at his bleeding body. Heidi buttoned her blouse and turned to Lieutenant Shroder.

"You did well," he told her.

She smiled modestly; in her heart, she was proud to be a German maiden, fighting for her country.

"Someone should come looking for these two pretty soon," Shroder said. "Let's get out of here."

SEVENTEEN

Mahoney glanced at his watch, wondering what had happened to Butsko and Kubiak. *They should have been back by now. Fucking assholes. Can't trust them with anything.*

Mahoney looked around at his men, who were smoking cigarettes and cleaning their rifles. He knew they ought to get back in the war, but they were low on ammunition, and where were Butsko and Kubiak? A sliver of pain throbbed above Mahoney's left eye, the result of the morning's tension. He thought it would be wonderful if he could relax someplace without worrying about ways to keep from getting killed. *Maybe I should move to the country when the war is over,* he thought. *Maybe I should become a farmer. Maybe Cranepool and I can do something together; he knows all about that stuff.*

He turned his thoughts to the problem at hand and decided that the only thing to do was take the men with him and try to find Cranepool.

"All right, saddle up!" he said getting to his feet.

"Where we going, sarge?" Pulaski asked.

"The find the first and second squads."

"What happened to Butsko and Kubiak?"

"How the fuck should I know?"

The men got up off the floor and put on their packs and cartridge belts. Riggs stood beside Mahoney, holding the walkie-talkie to his ear. Mahoney spat on the floor and cursed Butsko and Kubiak. He'd given them a simple task to do, and they'd fucked it up. He took out a piece of paper and wrote a message stating that he and the others had gone to look for the first and second squads, laying the message in the middle of the floor.

"Let's go," Mahoney said, "and don't bunch up."

They walked through the building and stepped out the rear door into a courtyard. Explosions were taking place a few blocks away, but the neighborhood around Mahoney was quiet. They entered the building behind the one they were in and found heaps of dead Germans lying around.

"Looks like Cranepool's work," Mahoney said.

They passed through that building and entered another, where they found more dead Germans. They made their way through several more buildings and finally heard explosions and gunfire next door.

Mahoney decided to take his men over there and investigate.

Cranepool charged into the attic, his carbine blazing and his teeth bared like a wild animal. German soldiers fired wildly at him, but he was a moving, dodging target, and his finger held the trigger back. His carbine bucked like an angry living thing in his hands, and the Germans fell at his feet, bleeding from wounds all over their bodies, as the room filled with smoke.

Germans entered the attic room from another door, and Cranepool cut them down with his carbine, enjoying the fight and sense of danger. When his carbine ran out of ammunition, he swung it around and used it like a baseball bat, rushing at Germans and battering them to the floor. Cranepool's men were behind him, and they shot whoever Cranepool missed.

Cranepool swung his carbine like a manic and felt exhilarated. The floor was greasy with blood, and part of somebody's brain was stuck to the front of his jacket, but he kept plowing into the Germans, who were crowded together and not eager to fight. All of Cranepool's pent-up frustrations and anger were turned loose on the Germans, and he felt as if he had become indestructible.

Finally, no Germans were standing in front of him. He flicked the bit of brain off his field jacket and looked around. His men stared at the bodies lying on the floor. Cranepool took off his helmet and wiped his forehead with his sleeve. He had captured some German hand grenades but was running out of rifle ammunition. He had no idea where he was and wished Mahoney was there to tell him how to proceed because he didn't want to stop and think about it himself.

"Somebody's coming up the stairs!" one of his men shouted.

Cranepool felt pleasure at the thought that more Germans were coming. He ejected the empty clip from his carbine and inserted a fresh one.

"We'll throw some grenades down their throats," he said, "and we'll see how they like that."

German hand grenades were fashioned like potato mashers with long wooden handles. Cranepool pulled one out of his boot and was about to arm it when he heard a familiar voice calling from below.

"Any Americans here!" shouted the voice.

"Isn't that Mahoney?" asked Private Croom.

Cranepool smiled. "It damn sure is!" He rushed toward the stairs and shouted down. "Mahoney, it's me—Cranepool!"

"Any krauts between you and me?"

"I don't think so!"

Cranepool heard Mahoney and his men trudge up the stairs, glad that Mahoney was there to help out with the fighting. Mahoney came into view on the stairs below, followed by eight men.

"Where's everybody else?" Cranepool asked.

"Dead or wounded," Mahoney replied. "How many you got left?"

"Ten."

"Shit." Mahoney climbed to the attic landing and looked at Cranepool's men. Nearly all the new replacements were missing. "How's your ammo situation?"

"Bad, but we found some of these." Cranepool held up a German hand grenade.

"Let's spread those grenades around, boys, because we don't have any."

Cranepool's men shared their grenades with the third and fourth squads, and Mahoney jammed the handle of one into his boot.

"I think we'd better go look for Captain Anderson," Mahoney said. "You eat yet?"

"A little while ago."

"Okay, let's go."

They descended the stairs and went out into the street, heading in the direction where they thought Captain Anderson might be. They heard explosions and sounds of bitter fighting in front of them, but to their rear all seemed placid. Patrols of soldiers marched toward the center of the city, and tanks rumbled over the streets, but evidently there wasn't much fighting in that neighborhood anymore.

Mahoney looked for familiar faces among the soldiers on the street but couldn't find anybody he knew. He decided that the battalion probably had moved toward the center of the city along with everybody else and headed in that general direction.

They turned a corner and saw army ambulances in front of a building. Orderlies unloaded wounded men from the vehicles, and a big white flag with a red cross upon it was hung out one of the windows. Mahoney and his platoon approached the building and noticed the numbers of his battalion and regiment stenciled on the bumper of one of the ambulances.

"Hey," Mahoney said to Cranepool, "that looks like our battalion aid station. Maybe somebody in there knows where Captain Anderson is."

They entered the building and saw that it was a gymnasium, its floor covered with bleeding American soldiers. Mahoney spotted an orderly and walked over to him, asking if he knew where Captain Anderson was.

The orderly pointed. "He was about six blocks that way last time I saw him."

"Thanks."

Mahoney stood up, making a mental note of where Captain Anderson was.

"Hey, sarge!" shouted Pulaski.

Mahoney spun around. "What now?"

"Look!" Pulaski pointed down at the crumpled body of a soldier. "It's Kubiak!"

Mahoney stepped over dead and wounded men, making his way toward Pulaski. The aid station smelled of antiseptic and intestines; doctors, nurses, and orderlies rushed about. Cranepool placed a lighted cigarette between the lips of a soldier he knew, and Private Gomez fed a friend of his a Hershey bar because the friend had no arms left.

Mahoney drew closer to Pulaski and looked down. Sure enough, it was Kubiak lying on the floor, stiff as a board.

"The Germans must have got him," Pulaski said.

Who the fuck else would have got him? Mahoney thought as he kneeled beside Kubiak. He saw the ugly stab wound in Kubiak's chest and noticed that Kubiak's shirt was half unbuttoned. *Why is his shirt like that?* Mahoney wondered. *Was he undressing?* Then Mahoney caught a whiff of perfume. At first, he didn't know where it was coming from, but as he bent closer to Kubiak, he realized that's where it was coming from. *What the hell's going on here?* Mahoney thought. *Did a broad kill him? And where's Butsko? Weren't they supposed to be together?*

"See if Butsko's around here!" Mahoney told his men.

They went to the part of the room where the dead bodies were stacked side by side. Mahoney walked along the rows, looking into the faces of dead soldiers. He recognized some of them, but death no longer astonished him or filled him with sadness. It had become a common occurrence.

"Here he is over here!" said Private, First Class Greene.

Mahoney strode toward Greene and looked at the bulky corpse at his feet. It was Butsko all right, shot to shit with bullets. Mahoney wondered what had happened to him. If he'd stayed on the street, he shouldn't have run into Germans. Where had he gone?

The survivors of the company gathered around Butsko. He hadn't been very popular because he'd been a bully, but now many of them felt solemn in the presence of his corpse. Mahoney didn't feel anything except surprise. He'd thought Butsko was a good soldier and couldn't imagine him walking into an ambush. Mahoney hadn't liked Butsko very much, but he didn't like most people, anyway. He thought it easier to deal with dead soldiers if he hadn't liked them when they were alive, so he made it a point not to like them.

Then he noticed that Butsko's shirt was partially unbuttoned, also. *What the fuck is going on here?* he wondered. He kneeled close to Butsko and sniffed around but couldn't detect any perfume.

"Does he stink already?" asked Pulaski.

Mahoney stood up and took out a cigarette. "Let's go find Captain Anderson," he said.

EIGHTEEN

Gen. Otto von Neubacher stood at the map table in his headquarters, located in a subterranean room beneath a public building in the center of the city. He noted the positions of his troops and the Americans and thought his troops were doing well considering that they didn't have access to reinforcements as the Americans did. He realized that despite his preparations and defense strategies, the Americans were too much for him. They would capture Metz eventually. it was only a matter of time.

"If only I had more tanks," he said to his chief of staff, Col. Rolf Knoedler.

"What would you do with them if you had them?" Knoedler asked. He wore wirerimmed eyeglasses and looked like a professor.

Neubacher stroked his Hitler moustache. "I would use them to break through the American lines and cut off their supplies. The Americans have expended a great deal of men and material to get where they are. If we could stop their replacements, we could stop them."

"Hmmm," said Knoedler, looking down at the map. "I can see your point. If we could have a few regiments of parachutists dropped on the other side of the Moselle, that would be ideal, but I don't suppose we could get a few regiments of parachutists, so it's all rather academic, isn't it?"

"Quite so," agreed Neubacher.

Also at the table was Lt. Franz Stahmer, only twenty-two years old and recently posted to the front after graduating from the University of Leipzig with a degree in mechanical engineering. "Sir, I have an idea," he said.

The older officers ignored him as they continued to discuss their precarious position vis-á-vis the Americans.

119

"Sir," Stahmer said louder, "I think I have a rather interesting idea."

They continued to ignore him while they spoke of troop withdrawals from exposed positions and maneuvers to straighten their lines. Stahmer, who was short and stout with straight black hair and a round moon face, felt angry at being neglected and disregarded.

"I believe," he said loudly, "that I have a way to get behind the American lines!"

All eyes turned to him.

"Who are you?" asked General Neubacher, adjusting his monocle as he studied Lieutenant Stahmer.

"Lieutenant Stahmer, sir!"

"Don't you know that you do not interrupt senior officers while they are in conference?" Neubacher turned to Knoedler and sighed. "It's really amazing, the caliber of young officer they send us these days."

"Indeed," agreed Knoedler.

Stahmer wasn't cowed by their attitude, for his father was a millionaire, and he was arrogant as only a millionaire's son can be.

"May I be permitted to present my point of view!" Stahmer said.

"If you must," Neubacher replied wearily.

Stahmer placed his finger on the map. "This is a railway line," he said. "It passes from the railroad station in the center of this city to points east, west, north, and south. The western route formerly extended to France over a bridge that spanned the Moselle River. That bridge has been bombed by the Americans, but as far as I know, the railroad line within the city limits is still more or less intact."

"Come now," Knoedler said, impatiently tapping his fingers on the table, "what is your point, lieutenant?"

"My point is that we can assemble a locomotive and some railway cars, or even a few locomotives and railway cars, load some of our best troops aboard, and in the middle of the night, when they least expect it, we send the trains west, have them smash through the American lines, and then unload the troops, which can proceed to cut the American supply columns and attack the Americans from the rear."

All the officers looked at the train line that led from the central station to the bridge over the Moselle River.

"Hmmm," said Neubacher, fingering his Hitler moustache. "I think you might have something here. What did you say your name was?"

"Lieutenant Franz Stahmer, sir."

"Yes, Stahmer. Well, we'll have to look into this more carefully. The principle problem, as I see it, is whether or not the track is open as far as the American lines. There's been quite a lot of bombing, you know."

"I know," said Stahmer.

"I think I'll put you in charge of this project since you've come up with the idea. We'll want to attack as soon as possible and at night so that we can't be stopped by their damned planes, so I'll expect your report within twenty-four hours. Can I rely on you, Stahmer?"

"Yes, sir."

"Good. You are dismissed."

Stahmer gave the Hitler salute and marched out of the room, passing SS Col. Anton Meier, the Gestapo commandant of Lorraine. Meier was lean as a jaguar, with a four-inch scar on his right cheek. He wore a black-leather trenchcoat and a black helmet with an SS insignia on the side. Tromping toward General Neubacher, he halted and gave the Hitler salute.

"What can I do for you?" Neubacher asked coolly, for he didn't like the SS commandant very much.

"I have developed an idea for the defense of this city, sir," Meier said. "It can win us a great victory, I believe."

The light of the electric lamp on the ceiling cast sharp shadows on Meier's craggy face. "There is presently in the city of Metz a shipment of poison gas called Zyklon B," he said. "I suggest that when the wind is right, we release the gas and let it destroy the Americans. My intelligence sources advise me that the Americans have thrown away their gas masks, so I imagine we might wipe the lot of them out,"— Meier snapped his fingers—"like that. What do you think?"

Neubacher looked at Knoedler in surprise. "I didn't know we had poison gas at the front."

"Neither did I," replied Knoedler.

Neubacher turned to Meier. "Are you sure there's poison gas here?"

"Quite sure."

"It's called Zyklon B, you say?"

"Yes, sir."

"What's it doing here?"

"It was on its way to the eastern front, sir."

"For what purpose?"

Meier smiled thinly. "For SS purposes. I'm afraid I cannot elaborate."

"Is poison gas being used against the Russians?" Neubacher asked.

"Not against Russian soldiers, no."

"Then what is it being used for?"

"I told you that I cannot elaborate," Meier said, because he didn't dare tell Neubacher that Zyklon B was used to kill Jews and gypsies in the concentration camps. That was top-secret SS information.

"Where is the gas now?" Neubacher asked.

"Somewhere," Meier replied mysteriously.

"I asked you *where!*"

"I cannot divulge that information, sir."

"Why not!"

"It is an SS matter entirely, sir. I offer you the gas for the defense of the city, but beyond that I have nothing to say."

"I see." Neubacher glanced at Knoedler. Both had been in the army long enough to know that the SS went its own way and wasn't subject to the army chain of command. Neubacher was worried about the Zyklon B because he thought Meier and his SS goons were a bunch of maniacs. Neubacher decided to deal with the matter diplomatically for the time being.

"Thank you for your offer, Colonel Meier," he said. "If I decide to take you up on it, I'll let you know. I trust the Zyklon B is in a safe place, where it cannot be disturbed by American artillery or bombs?"

"Of course."

"I'll contact you if I need to use the stuff."

"Very good."

Meier rendered the Hitler salute and marched out of the

conference room. Neubacher looked at Knoedler. "I'd certainly like to know where that gas is," he said.

"So would I."

"Is there any way we might find out?"

"I don't think so. SS men are tighter than clams."

Knoedler touched his fingers to his chin. "I'd feel a lot better if I knew where that gas was."

"So would I. There's no telling what those fools might do with it."

Mahoney found Captain Anderson in a schoolhouse with fifty soldiers wearing new green fatigues.

"They're new replacements," Anderson said. "Every platoon will get about a dozen of them."

Mahoney looked the replacements over, and they appeared frightened and uncertain. This was the closest they'd ever been to combat, and didn't know what to expect.

"I'm expecting the new orders from battalion," Anderson said. "Sit tight until they arrive."

"Yes, sir," Mahoney said. "By the way, did Butsko and Kubiak ever get through to you?"

"Yes," Anderson replied. "I gave them some ammo and hand grenades. I told Butsko to tell you to join all your squads together and try to link up with the second platoon. Didn't he get through to you?"

"He got through to the Graves Registration squad. He's dead. Kubiak, too."

"Dead?" Anderson asked, surprised.

"Yes."

"I wonder what happened to them?"

"So do I."

Anderson was called to the field telephone by Private, First Class Drago, and Mahoney sat on the floor with his back to a wall, taking out a cigarette. They were in a classroom filled with tiny desks and chairs, and none of the men could fit on the chairs, but some of them sat on the desks and used the chairs for footstools.

Mahoney puffed his cigarette and thought about Butsko and Kubiak. He guessed that the perfume he'd smelled on Kubiak probably came from one of the nurses in the aid station, and both their shirts probably had been unbuttoned by nurses or medics as part of an examination. Mahoney decided he'd been foolish to think that Butsko and Kubiak had been with women. *I'm always thinking about sex,* Mahoney said to himself. *Why am I always thinking about sex?*

Captain Anderson hung up his field telephone and turned to Mahoney. "I've got something for you to do, sergeant."

"What is it this time?" Mahoney asked, getting to his feet. He sauntered over to where Anderson was.

"There's a big church down the street," Anderson said, "and some Germans are holed up in it. We don't want to blow the church up because it's been there for a few hundred years, so somebody will have to go in and kill the Germans."

"Is that somebody gonna be the first platoon?"

"Right. Germans snipers are up in the steeple, and nobody can move in the streets below except tanks. You've got to get those snipers out of there."

"Personally," Mahoney said, "I think they ought to blow up the church."

"How can you say that, Mahoney? I thought you were a Catholic."

"The church is only a building. If we blow it up, they'll build another one. What's the matter with that?"

"They don't want to blow it up. It's too old. Your platoon and fifteen of the new men ought to be enough. Any questions?"

"No, sir."

Mahoney picked fifteen of the new men and assigned them to the squads of his platoon, nearly bringing it up to full strength again. Cranepool still was leader of the first squad, Private, First Class Stafford became leader of the second, Pulaski replaced Butsko as leader of the third, and Private, First Class Croom was named leader of the fourth.

"Let's go," said Mahoney

They stepped on to the sidewalk, bandoliers of ammunition hanging from their shoulders and hand grenades in their pockets. They were not under fire until they turned the first corner and looked down a wide avenue to the church at its end, about four hundred yards down the street. The street was clogged with tanks, and men fired at the church from doorways and windows. It was an old Gothic church with tall spires and flying buttresses, decorated with gargoyles. Puffs of smoke emitted from the belfry where German snipers were firing at American soldiers.

Mahoney deployed his men in doorways and behind tanks as he tried to figure out a plan of action. Somehow he and his men would have to get inside the church, and the only way to do that would be to blow some doors down. However, that was probably what the Germans expected, and you don't want to do what your enemy expects. Mahoney raised his binoculars and gazed at the church through them. There probably was a back door behind the church, but the Germans must have that guarded, also. The only thing to do was to go in through the stained-glass windows, most of which appeared to be blown out. The windows were high off the ground. How could they get through them? Mahoney looked at the tanks. Maybe he could use the tanks for ladders and shelter.

He left his doorway and trotted to the first tank, banging on the hull with his rifle butt. A head popped out of the turret and asked what Mahoney wanted. Mahoney said he needed to talk to the person in charge of the tanks. A hand came out of the turret and pointed to a tank on the other side of the street.

Mahoney ran across the street and climbed up on the tank. He bent over the open turret and shouted: "Who's in charge here!"

A scowling face beneath a tanker's helmet appeared in the metallic gloom below. "Who wants to know?"

"My name's Master Sergeant Mahoney. I need some tank support because I've got to take that church up ahead."

The man in the helmet climbed the ladder and looked out of the turret at the church. "We've been told not to fire at the church. It's famous."

"You can shoot your machine guns, can't you?"

"Yeah, provided we don't break anything. Our fifty calibers really tear the shit out of things, you know."

"Well, basically," Mahoney said, "we just want to hide behind the tanks until we get to the church, and then we want to climb up and go through the windows. You can do that for us, can't you?"

"I suppose," the man said. "How soon will you be ready to move out?"

"About five minutes."

"That should be enough time."

Mahoney returned to his platoon, took them inside a building, and told them what to do. He said that once they got inside the church, they should spread out quickly and kill the Germans. He and Cranepool would take the first squad and get the snipers in the steeple. He told his men that they should be cautious but at the same time move fast. "Any questions?"

A big man with narrow shoulders and a fat gut raised his hand. "How can we be cautious and go fast at the same time?" he asked in a Southern drawl.

"What's your name?" Mahoney asked.

"Private Cruikshank."

"You just go as fast as you can, but watch your ass. You understand that?"

"I think so, sergeant."

There were no more questions. Mahoney led them out into the street and deployed them behind the tanks. He banged on the hull of the tank belonging to the officer in charge, who came up with his brow furrowed.

"We're ready to roll," Mahoney told him.

"So are we." The officer spoke into the mouthpiece of his headset. "Move it out!"

The tanks rumbled down the cobblestone street. Soldiers hiding in doorways watched Mahoney and his men pass. The buildings along the avenue were half destroyed, and the tanks went around huge shell craters. Mahoney looked over the tank at the church up ahead. He could see life-sized statues of the saints around the doors. It really was a beautiful church, but he wondered if it was worth one human life.

The Germans in the church saw the tanks coming and fired at them and the men hovering behind them. The tanks fired a few bursts from their .50-caliber machine guns, tearing chunks of marble off the building, and Mahoney and his men fired their rifles at the puffs of smoke on the steeple and in the windows. *The Germans must know we're coming*, he thought. *They'll fight harder than ever now.*

The tanks drew closer to the church and veered to the right side of it. Mahoney looked up at the steeple and saw objects falling through the air.

"Hand grenades coming down!" he yelled. "Take cover!"

The men looked up, and the green ones didn't know which way to go. Some tried to crawl under the moving tanks, others ran for shelter and were cut down by the snipers. Mahoney stayed close to the tank and tried to get some metal between him and the hand grenades. They exploded in midair, sending shrapnel flying in all directions, ricocheting off the tanks and cutting down a few of the GIs.

The tanks continued to roll to the side of the church and soon were out of range of the Germans in the steeple, but Germans fired out of the broken stained-glass windows on the side of the church.

The tanks inched closer to the windows. Mahoney and his men threw grenades through the windows, then climbed on to the tanks and jumped. They burst through the jagged glass openings, covering their faces with their arms, and landing among the pews and granite columns inside the church.

At first, there was chaos as Germans rushed toward that side of the church and opened fire and the GIs tried to pick themselves up from the floor. Shattered German bodies lay beneath the windows, the victims of the hand grenades.

Mahoney, on one knee, hid behind a pew and fired his carbine on automatic at the Germans, his head filled with memories of his Catholic childhood in Hell's Kitchen and his days as a choirboy at Saint Paul's. Never had he dreamed that he'd be killing people in a church, but that's what he was doing.

A German raised his head behind a pew, and Mahoney simultaneously fired a burst at him, tearing off the top of the German's head. Another German threw a grenade at Mahoney, who dodged to the side, ran three paces, and dived between two pews. The grenade went off, making the floor quiver and echoing across the vast expanse of the church. Mahoney threw a grenade of his own in the direction from which the German grenade had come and ducked down again. The grenade made a terrific blast, and portions of German bodies were thrown into the air.

Mahoney saw that his platoon had the Germans outnumbered. "Forward!" he yelled, "keep moving forward!"

His men crawled through pews and hid behind statues of saints, firing at the Germans who seemed to be withdrawing in the direction of the altar.

"Stay after them!" Mahoney cried, firing his carbine from behind a pillar that went all the way up to the ceiling of the church. While changing clips in his carbine, he glanced up and saw angels and stars painted on the ceiling. He almost felt like getting down on his knees and saying a Hail Mary and an Our Father because that's the way churches affected him, but this was no time for foolishness.

Mahoney and his men kept pressing the Germans, who continued to retreat toward the altar, which was huge and magnificent, made of white marble, and showing the crucified Christ surrounded by saints, angels, and crowds of people dressed in the garb of the sixteenth century. Mahoney advanced through a row of pews, turned a corner, and saw a German officer lying on the floor, blood leaking from his stomach and a pistol in his hand, aiming shakily at Mahoney. The officer gritted his teeth and pulled the trigger, and a bullet whistled past Mahoney's ear. Mahoney aimed down and pulled the trigger of his carbine, spraying the German officer with hot lead and sending him into convulsions.

Mahoney stepped over him and saw German's run behind the altar, where they took positions and fired at the GIs from behind statues of Jesus and the saints. Mahoney hid behind a baptismal font and raked the altar with his carbine on automatic fire. Chips of marble flew into the air, and one German screamed as a lucky bullet passed between the head of the Virgin Mary and Saint Veronica to lodge in the chest of the German.

Mahoney was out of ammunition again. He crouched behind the baptismal font and fed a new clip into his carbine, thinking that he'd been baptized once in a font very much like this one and probably looked like one of the cherubs carved into the altar from behind which Germans were shooting at him.

"Oh, fuck," Mahoney muttered, raising his carbine to his shoulder and firing at the Germans behind the altar. One German appeared to be climbing up the back of the altar so he could fire down at the GIs. Mahoney took a few shots at him, but the bullets ricocheted off the white marble.

The church filled with boiling clouds of gunsmoke. Mahoney decided that the only way to get those Germans was to charge the altar in waves, one squad advancing while the other squads furnished cover.

"First squad, forward!" Mahoney yelled. "The rest of you maintain your fire!"

Cranepool led his first squad forward, skipping around the pews and dashing up the aisles. The German climbing the altar reached the top and aimed his rifle down, but Mahoney had been waiting for him to expose himself and fired one careful shot at the German's face. It split apart, and the German tumbled over the top of the structure, falling to his back on the altar below, where he lay with his arms spread out and his blood leaking down over the white marble.

"Second squad, forward!" Mahoney said, looking at the German's blood running down in crimson rivulets. *The blood of the lamb*, Mahoney thought.

The second squad charged down the side aisle to take the Germans on the flank. They hid in the front row of pews, and then Mahoney ordered the third squad forward. A German leaned around a corner of the altar and threw a hand grenade, which bounced on the floor, rolled under the pew, and sent the GI's scurrying for cover. The grenade exploded, blowing the pew and two GIs into the air, and the rest of the second squad, with nowhere else to go, charged toward the side of the altar, with Private, First Class Stafford out in front, a hand grenade of his own in his hand. He hurled it and dived to the floor. The Germans saw it come, tried to catch it, and nervously bobbled it. It exploded in their faces, taking off their heads and arms.

The third squad charged down the aisle on the other side of the altar and attacked the remaining Germans from behind, shooting them in their backs. A few of the Germans ran away through a door behind the altar, but the rest of them were slaughtered by the GIs coming at them from both sides. The first squad, led by Cranepool, went after the Germans who'd gone through the door.

It became silent in the church except for the shots high up in the steeple. Mahoney walked through the gunsmoke, a dazed look on his face, toward the altar where the dead German lay in front of the little doors where the host ordinarily would be stored. Mahoney wasn't very religious anymore, but he never dreamed that one day he'd kill a man on the altar of a church. The German's blood made crimson rivulets down the white marble and formed pools on the floor.

As Mahoney approached, he could see that the soldier was around thirty and hadn't shaved for a few days. Mahoney's hair stood on end when he realized that the German looked just like paintings he'd seen of Jesus, and he, Mahoney, had killed him. He dropped to his knees in front of the altar and crossed himself.

"You okay, sarge?" Pulaski asked, walking up to Mahoney.

Mahoney stood and stared at the German. "He looks just like Christ," Mahoney said.

"Naw, he don't," Pulaski replied. "He looks like a fucking kraut to me."

Mahoney looked at Pulaski and smiled. "Yeah, you're right. He's just a fucking kraut, right?"

"Right."

Mahoney looked toward the ceiling and the sounds of gunfire. "Now let's get the cocksuckers up there."

Mahoney tried to remember how one got to the steeple at Saint Paul's in New York but couldn't remember. It had been a long time ago, and he probably hadn't known it then, either.

"I want you squad leaders to take your men and look for the way to the fucking belfry. It's probably back by the sacristy."

"What's a sacristy?" Cruikshank asked.

Mahoney looked at Pulaski. "Tell him what a sacristy is and get him the fuck away from me."

"Hup, sarge."

The squad leaders took their men away, and Mahoney sat on the stairs to the altar, lighting up a cigarette. Riggs sat nearby, trying to be quiet so he wouldn't disturb Mahoney, and Grossberger was out in the pews, attending to the wounded.

Mahoney puffed his cigarette, feeling satisfied with himself. They'd cleared out the church in record time and soon would take care of the snipers in the steeple. Not too many of his men had been killed. Soon the streets would be clear, and the other GIs could move up.

Something compelled Mahoney to turn around, and he saw the German lying on the altar, his blood still oozing down the white marble. Mahoney felt overcome with sorrow, as if he were one of the soldiers who'd killed Christ. He knew that was irrational, but somehow, on a deeper level, he thought it was absolutely correct. He turned away and scratched the growth of beard on his face, getting angry with himself. *What's the matter with me?* he thought. *Am I going nuts? Have I finally got combat fatigue?* Once again, he turned around and looked at the bleeding German. *I only did what I had to do. Get off my fucking back.*

Then he remembered Saint Paul's and became angry. *Those damned priests and nuns messed up my mind when I was a little kid!* he thought. *They're the ones who did this to me!* He stood up and paced back and forth in front of the altar. The German's helmet lay on the floor, and he kicked it into the air. *I didn't ask to be a soldier,* Mahoney thought. *Those fucking priests made me feel guilty about everything.*

He stopped suddenly because he realized why he was mad. It wasn't the priests, he just was making them into scapegoats. It was because he actually felt he'd done something wrong this time. He saw that German not as the enemy but as a young man like Christ who was killed in anger, this time by him.

Mahoney put his hands to the sides of his head because he could feel the pressure building inside. One part of him was a soldier trained to kill, and another part of him cried out that killing was wrong. *If we don't kill them, they'll kill us,* Mahoney thought. *If I turn the other cheek, they'll kill me. Why should I let them do that? I want to live! What about eternal life?* asked the little voice in his mind.

Mahoney snarled and kicked the altar, nearly breaking his toe. "Son of a bitch bastard!" he screamed.

"You call me, sarge?" asked Riggs, who had been sitting nearby and becoming increasingly worried about Mahoney.

"No, I didn't call you!"

"You okay, sarge?"

"Yeah, I'm okay!"

"I think the devils have got you."

"If you don't shut up, *I'm* going to get *you!*"

"Hup, sarge."

Mahoney paced back and forth behind the altar, his hands clasped behind his back. *Those goddamned priests,* he thought. *They did this to me. If I ever get back to New York alive, I'll go to Saint Paul's and really kick ass.*

Pulaski ran up to Mahoney. "Sarge, we found the way to the belfry."

"Where is it?"

Pulaski pointed to the front of the church. "There's steps over there."

Mahoney cupped his hands around his mouth and told everybody to follow him. Then he stomped to the front of the church and went up a few flights of stairs to an airy room that had the ropes of the bells hanging down into it and a metal spiral staircase leading up to where the Germans were.

Mahoney wondered how they were going to get at the German snipers; if he or his men tried to climb the spiral staircase, the Germans would shoot them from above. The staircase was enclosed by the stone structure of the spire, and it was so tall that he doubted if a hand grenade thrown by the Germans would make it all the way down before exploding.

"Well," Pulaski said, "we can wait until they run out of ammunition or food."

"No," replied Mahoney, "they might kill a lot more GIs before then. Do they know we're here?"

"I don't know."

Mahoney tiptoed toward the bell ropes and looked up the concrete shaft. He could see some sky and the system of bells, and the sound of German gunfire echoed down to him through the shaft. Pulling back, he wrinkled his forehead and wondered how to get the Germans down from there.

"I got another idea, sarge," Pulaski said.

"What is it this time, asshole?"

"I think Corporal Cranepool's got a grenade launcher with him, and you can use it to shoot a grenade up there and maybe kill all the krauts." Pulaski smiled as if he'd just discovered a new secret weapon.

Mahoney shook his head. "Maybe that'll blow the steeple off this church, too, and we're not supposed to do that, right?"

"We'll say we couldn't help it."

"And they'll say you'll all be minus a stripe from now on. No, there's got to be a better way."

Riggs raised his finger in the air. "I've got an idea," he said hesitantly.

"Oh-oh," Mahoney replied. "Riggs has got an idea. Watch out."

"I really have got an idea," Riggs said, "and I'll bet it'll work."

"Let's hear it," Mahoney told him.

"Well," Riggs said, "loud sounds can make people crazy, and—"

Mahoney interupted him. "Is that how you went crazy?"

"No, I went crazy because I used to see my father screwing my sister, but to get back to what I was saying about sound, you know that big church bells make a lot of noise, and if we were to pull those ropes and get those bells ringing, I don't think the krauts up there would like it very much."

Mahoney looked at Riggs as though he'd never seen him before. "You know, that's not a bad idea, Riggs."

"I told you it was a good idea, sarge, but you don't listen to me because you're too busy listening to the devils all the time, and not the good devils, either, but the bad devils."

Mahoney looked at the ropes hanging around the room. "I want three men on each one of those ropes, and when I give the word, I want you to heave with all you've got."

The men rushed around the room and grabbed ropes, looking at Mahoney, who unslung his carbine and opened the chamber to make sure there was a round inside.

"Are you all ready?" Mahoney asked.

They nodded as sounds of gunfire continued to reverberate down the shaft.

"Hit it!" Mahoney said.

The men pulled the ropes, hanging the full weight of their bodies on them, and from the top of the steeple came the sound of bells pealing. The sound was so loud that the walls of the room seemed to vibrate, and Mahoney was tempted to stick his fingers in his ears, but he had to be ready for the Germans. The GIs heaved and pulled the ropes, while above them the bells swung back and forth, sometimes doing complete somersaults, ringing with a sound that rattled the marrow of their bones.

In the steeple, the German snipers panicked. They dropped their rifles and pressed their hands against their ears, grimacing and looking for someplace to hide; the bells were causing agonizing pain in their ears and heads. They looked at each other wildly, wondering what to do and unable to think clearly because of the noise. Their eardrums burst and blood ran out of their ears.

They realized their only hope was to get out of that steeple, and they didn't care what was waiting for them below. They ran toward the spiral staircase and descended it rapidly, every step taking them a little farther from the monstrous sounds.

But every step brought them closer to Mahoney. He waited until he thought all of them were on the spiral staircase, and then, moving quickly, he positioned himself on one knee and fired his carbine up on automatic while the bells continued to toll.

The Germans screamed in horror, but the bells drowned out the sounds of their voices. Some were killed immediately and fell down the spiral staircase, and others tried to climb back up again, but Mahoney's bullets were faster than they. The bullets ripped into the bottoms of their feet and their groins.

Mahoney stepped back and watched the Germans fall at his feet. He looked up the staircase and could see a few Germans up there, still twitching. He held up his hand, and the GIs stopped pulling the ropes. Gradually, the sounds of bells diminished. When they were silent, Mahoney sent two squads up the staircase to polish off any Germans who still might be alive on the roof.

The GIs climbed the staircase, and Mahoney searched the Germans on the floor for money and valuables. He found two good gold watches, giving one to Riggs, and liberated some German marks, which he intended to save so that he'd have something to spend when the Hammerheads entered Germany.

He heard a sound behind him and spun around, raising his carbine. It was Cranepool, leading his squad up the stairs. Cranepool held his canteen out to Mahoney and had a dizzy smile on his face.

"Hey, sarge," Cranepool said, his face flushed and his breath smelling like a saloon, "there's a shitload of wine in the cellar, and it's pretty good. Have some."

Mahoney snatched the canteen from Cranepool's hand and brought it to his lips. He threw his head back and swallowed some of the wine, which was fiery and sweet, just like when he was a choirboy at St. Paul's.

"There's a lot of this down there, you say?" Mahoney asked.

"More than we can drink in a week."

"No shit?"

"No shit."

"Well, then," Mahoney said, licking his lips, "I think that maybe we'd all better take a little break down in that cellar."

NINETEEN

It was night in Metz, and the artillery barrage continued. It was raining again, and the air was thick with smoke. A faint glow could be seen above the rooftops as portions of the city burned.

At eleven o'clock, Lt. Franz Stahmer left the central railroad yards at the head of two platoons of engineers. They all wore raincoats and steel helmets, and some of the engineers, who'd never seen Stahmer before, joked about how fat he was.

They made their way over the network of tracks, heading west toward the line that formerly carried trains to Paris. Much of the track in the yard had been destroyed by bombing, but Stahmer was able to work out a route whereby trains could leave the yard and go west. He and his engineers followed this route out of the yard toward the front lines.

Stahmer walked at the head of the engineers, carrying his note pad and pencil, kicking rails and crossties, making sure the tracks could carry trains. He hoped that the tracks were serviceable because if his plan worked and the defenders of Metz could defeat the Americans, he'd become a hero and probably be promoted to captain.

They came to a section where a bomb had destroyed a length of track, and Stahmer made a note of it. Work parties would come later to fix the track, using rails cannibalized from other lines. Farther on, they reached another section that had been slightly damaged, and Stahmer made his customary notation.

They passed through the center of Metz, which the Germans still held. Gradually, the sound of fighting came closer, and occasionally a shell would hurtle to earth like a comet, forcing them to drop on to their stomachs. They'd get to their feet after the shell exploded and continue along the tracks.

Slowly, they drew closer to the American lines. The sounds of fighting increased in intensity, and more bombs fell around them. Stahmer knew now that the track had not been damaged very badly. A few nights of work should be enough to make the line operational, and then they could launch their sneak attack. The Americans never would expect it. They'd be outflanked before they knew it.

Suddenly, Stahmer heard footsteps up ahead and stopped cold. His men heard the footsteps, too, and unslung their rifles. They all crouched, waiting to see whether their own soldiers or Americans were coming toward them; if they were Americans, they'd open fire.

Figures emerged out of the night wearing the black uniforms of the SS. Stahmer was relieved and stood up. "Hello there!" he said, noticing a blonde young woman among them.

"Hello!" said the leader of the SS men, a husky lieutenant. "Who goes there!"

"An engineering patrol," replied Stahmer, "and you?"

"A death squad."

"Death squad?" Stahmer asked as the SS men drew closer. "What's a death squad?"

Lieutenant Shroder smiled as he approached. "We ambush and kill American soldiers. What are you doing out here?"

"Oh, nothing," replied Stahmer, because his railroad project was top secret.

"Nothing?" asked Shroder. "Well, carry on."

The SS men and the blonde woman passed by on their way to the center of Metz. Stahmer watched them go, wondering what they used the woman for; then he turned around and resumed his task of inspecting the rail line.

The first platoon of Charlie Company slept soundly in the cellar of the church, surrounded by barrels of wine tilted on to their sides. They'd gorged themselves on the wine, and some had spilled it all over their clothes. Puddles of wine were on the floor, and the subterranean room stank terribly, but the men snored with smiles on their faces. They'd stacked barrels of wine against the door so that no one would disturb them because no one was fit to stand guard throughout the night.

Mahoney was the first to awake, and after rubbing his eyes and yawning, he checked his watch. It was six o'clock in the morning, and it occurred to him that Captain Anderson might be awfully worried about them. He might even have the first platoon listed as missing in action on the morning report, and then there'd be some explaining to do.

"All right, you scumbags!" he yelled. "On your feet!"

The men stirred and snarled. They yawned, and some of them stumbled into dark corners to take leaks.

"Let's go!" Mahoney said. "We've got to report in!"

Cranepool stood up, his hands holding his head. "Oh my God, I don't think I can make it."

"You'll make it—don't worry."

Riggs staggered about, his tongue hanging out of his mouth. "Ooohhhhhh."

"Shaddup, you fucking asshole, and pick up that walkie-talkie."

Mahoney finally got the men organized. They unstacked the barrels in front of the door and left the cellar, climbing into the church, which was beginning to smell rank because of the dead German bodies. Leaving the church through a side door, they saw the first glimmer of dawn on the horizon. It was a chilly morning, and they huddled inside their field jackets, wishing they had some water to drink as they followed Mahoney back to the front lines.

Patton strode into his conference room, his uniform neatly pressed and necktie positioned correctly between the points of his collar. His boots were freshly polished, and he slapped his riding crop against his leg.

"How's the attack going?" he asked Col. Maddox, who was standing next to the map table with a sheaf of papers in his hand.

"Steady progress is being made on all fronts," Maddox replied.

"What about Metz?"

"I have the latest positions marked on the map."

Patton strode toward the map table and looked down. He

could see that the Hammerhead Division had taken approximately 20 percent of the city in the first day of fighting.

"They're not moving fast enough," Patton said. "I'd better call Donovan and light a fire under his ass."

"The Germans are putting up stiff resistance," Maddox said.

"Then the Hammerheads will have to fight harder."

Patton marched toward the communications center, holding out his hand. The sergeant in charge handed him a telephone.

"Get me General Donovan," Patton said gruffly.

Col. Anton Meier sat behind his desk in Gestapo headquarters in Metz, drinking a cup of coffee made out of real coffee beans. His desk was littered with communiqués from SS units in the front lines of the Metz battle, and they disheartened him. The Americans were making slow but steady progress. It would only be a matter of time before they captured the city. Meier would become a prisoner of the Americans in a few days if he didn't flee the city, and he had no intention of fleeing the city because Himmler would have him shot if he did.

On the other hand, if the Americans took him prisoner, he would be in for a bad time. They'd find the torture chambers beneath the headquarters building and would be outraged by them. They'd also find mutilated corpses and maybe even some prisoners who'd managed to escape. The prisoners would tell horror stories about the activities of the SS in Metz under the command of Colonel Meier. They might put him before a firing squad right away or even turn him over to the French underground, which would be worse.

Meier lit a cigarette and blew smoke out of the corner of his mouth. The only thing for him to do would be to die at his post in Metz. That prospect didn't bother him particularly because it would be a hero's death. They might even erect a statue to him someday in his home town of Bremen. He was a fanatical SS man, and for him there were things worse than death, such as disgrace or treachery. Moreover, he belonged to a special sect of SS officers who practiced occult rites and believed in reincarnation, so he thought that his death wouldn't be an end at all but a new beginning.

His ace in the hole was the shipment of Zyklon B hidden in

a basement room of Gestapo headquarters. Regardless of what General Neubacher had said, Meier fully intended to unleash the Zyklon B on the Americans when they got close enough to Gestapo headquarters. The Zyklon B was extremely deadly, and one good whiff of it could kill a man. It would kill everyone in the blocks surrounding Gestapo headquarters before it dissipated into the air. It might even kill everyone for miles around, and how wonderful that would be. Metz would become a vast cemetery, and in years to come it would be written that Colonel Meier of the SS had wiped out huge numbers of the Americans while sacrificing his life at the same time. The *Fuehrer* and Himmler would give speeches praising his name. There'd be parades and special ceremonies. City squares would be named after him. Songs would be composed about his heroic last stand.

Meier couldn't sit still behind his desk, so excited was he by the prospects of glory after his death. He rose and paced the floor, the cup of coffee in his hand, sipping and thinking about future party rallies at Nuremburg, where the *Fuehrer* would praise his great sacrifice. How Meier had loved those big party rallies. He'd been to every one of them since 1928, when he'd joined the party.

The telephone on his desk buzzed, snapping him out of his reverie. He picked up the phone. "Yes?"

"Lieutenant Shroder is here to see you, sir."

"Send him right in."

"Yes, sir."

The door opened, and Lieutenant Shroder marched into the office, wearing his black SS uniform and carrying his helmet underneath his arm. "Heil Hitler!" he cried.

"Heil Hitler!" Meier looked Shroder up and down, pleased by what he saw. Shroder also was a fanatical SS man and an idealist like himself. He was blond, had a square jaw, and surely was a pure Aryan of the very finest quality. He was leader of one of the special killer squads organized by Meier to ambush and kill American soldiers. "Have a seat, Shroder," Meier said.

"I prefer to stand, sir!"

"But you deserve a rest after all the fine work I'm sure you're doing."

"No one should rest until this city is cleared of Americans," Shroder replied.

"Quite," agreed Meier. "Well, I'll stand, too, then. What have you to report?"

"My squad has killed twenty-six American soldiers, sir."

"Very good," said Meier, puffing his cigarette. "And how many of your men have you lost?"

"Only three, sir."

"An excellent ratio. Your girl is holding up well—what is her name?"

"Heidi, sir."

"Yes, Heidi. How about her?"

"She's doing very well, sir. The Americans cannot resist her."

"I can understand why. She's a lovely young thing. How fortunate you are to be able to spend so much time with her."

Shroder blushed. "Yes, sir. We have returned to base because we need more ammunition. Then we shall go out into the city again."

"Are you sure you wouldn't like to wear civilian clothes instead of uniforms?" Meier asked. "Don't you think you're more conspicuous in your uniforms?"

"We are soldiers, sir, not terrorists. We prefer to wear our uniforms."

"I can understand that," Meier said. "I'd do the same myself if I were you."

TWENTY

Three days later, the railroad line between the center of the city and the American lines was repaired. The fighting still was bitter, and the Americans continued to make steady gains. That evening, Generals Neubacher and Knoedler visited the railway yards to inspect the preparations for the train attack to be made later in the night. It was raining again, and their boots stuck in the muck as they walked across the yard.

They entered one of the huge buildings and in the dimness saw railroad cars being attached to two locomotives. Lieutenant Stahmer was supervising, and when he saw Neubacher and Knoedler, he rushed toward them and saluted.

"How's everything going?" Neubacher asked.

"Excellently, sir."

"Do you have sufficient railroad cars?"

"Yes, sir. We'll be able to transport two battalions through the American lines."

"Very good. Are you sure the tracks are still intact, because the Americans bombed again today, you know."

"I have a work party out there right now."

Neubacher smiled and slapped Stahmer on the shoulder. "You've done a fine job, lieutenant. I suppose you'll want to join the attack?"

"Me?" asked Stahmer, because he wanted no such thing.

"Yes. I imagine that since you've done so much work, you'd want to participate in the attack."

Stahmer smiled nervously. "That's true—I would. But I have so many important and significant things to do that I don't think I'll have the time."

"Nonsense," said Neubacher. "We'll make time for you.

After all, who would have more of a right to engage in this attack than you?"

Stahmer tried to smile. "Thank you, sir. That would be most kind of you."

Neubacher smiled. "Think nothing of it. It's the least we can do for you. Are the troops nearby?"

"Yes, sir. In the buildings surrounding this yard. They can't wait to get going."

"They're the officer candidates, aren't they?"

"Yes, sir."

"They're just about the best troops we have in Metz right now. If they can't cut off the American supply lines, nobody can. When will you have everything in readiness, Lieutenant Stahmer?"

"A few hours before dawn, sir. I'd guess two o'clock in the morning."

"Excellent. If there are any problems, contact me directly."

"Yes, sir."

"That is all. Carry on."

The rifle shot rang out, and Mahoney noted the location of the muzzle blast. It was straight ahead and about two stories up in the air. The night became silent again. Mahoney crouched behind the pile of rubble and tried to figure a way to move forward without being seen.

There was a sniper up there, shooting at whatever American targets were presented to him. Captain Anderson had sent Mahoney forward to get the sniper, who shot three men and one officer since dusk. Mahoney was selected because he was supposed to be good at this sort of thing.

Mahoney's face and hands were blackened with camouflage paint, and the shiny metallic parts of his carbine had been coated with the stuff, too. Mahoney paused behind the rubble, savoring his solitude, for he was usually surrounded by men looking to him for solutions to problems. Now he was alone in no man's land, he and the sniper. One of them would be dead before long.

He got down on his belly and began crawling, his carbine cradled in his arms. Beneath him was pavement covered with broken bricks and stones that bruised his elbows and knees. He crept behind walls standing alone in the nightmare landscape and beside piles of wood and bricks that had once been buildings. Occasionally, he saw an arm or a leg sticking out of rubble. Rain pinged off his helmet and dripped down his back. He thought of himself as a hunter on the trail of the most wily prey of all, another human being.

The sniper fired again. Mahoney saw the muzzle blast out of the corner of his eye and kept moving, wondering if the sniper had killed another GI. Mahoney wondered what kind of man the sniper was to permit himself to occupy a lonely position in no man's land and spend the night trying to kill men five hundred yards away.

Mahoney crawled across a cobblestone street and around more piles of rubble. This part of the city had been devastated by artillery fire during the day, and thin trails of smoke rose all around him. Sometimes he'd touch piles of bricks that still were warm. Gradually, over a period of an hour, he covered the final distance and stopped fifty yards from the building where the sniper was holed up.

It was five stories high, and huge slabs of its walls were missing. It stood alone, surrounded by piles of rubble and planks of wood sticking into the air. Mahoney couldn't pinpoint which floor the sniper was on. He figured it probably was the top floor or even the roof, but he wasn't sure. He hoped the sniper would fire again so he could see.

Lying on bricks and stones, he gazed steadily at the building, waiting for the sniper to fire again. He wished he could have a cigarette and was getting hungry. Little dots of light appeared in his vision, and he realized he was straining his eyes. The manuals said that night fighters must keep moving their eyes around and never look directly at what they wanted to see because at night peripheral vision was more accurate than direct vision.

The sniper fired again, and Mahoney saw exactly where he was: on the fifth floor and two windows in from the right. *You're as good as dead, you kraut fucker,* Mahoney thought, crawling forward.

He circled around so that he'd approach the building from the side where the sniper couldn't see him. Then he moved stealthily toward the building. Closer and closer he came, and when he was almost there, the sniper fired another shot. Mahoney stopped cold and thought a bullet was entering his back, but it was only his imagination, and he continued crawling toward the building.

He reached it and stood up, pressing his back to the wall. Listening and looking around, he heard only the crackle of rifle fire in the distance and an occasional explosion. Nothing moved in the darkness. He moved sideways around the corner and made his way to the back door of the building.

Reaching the back door, he paused again for a few moments, then slipped inside. He saw a flight of stairs and climbed them silently to the main hall of the building. Ahead, he could see the front door. Another shot rang out above him, and he thought he'd better get that sniper quickly before he killed any more people.

He climbed the stairs, holding his carbine so that it pointed straight ahead. Every few steps he stopped and listened, but he heard nothing. His progress was slow, but he'd learned in the Rangers that it was better to take your time than rush into a hail of bullets.

He reached the first-floor landing and climbed to the second floor, thinking that people had once lived in this building, drinking coffee, listening to the radio, and fucking. Now it was deserted, and all the windows were gone. Piles of plaster were everywhere, broken loose from the walls by artillery shells landing nearby.

He passed the second floor and went up to the third. The sniper fired again, and Mahoney wondered if he was aiming at targets or just trying to harass the Americans. Well, he wouldn't do it much longer. Mahoney held his finger over the trigger of his carbine and tiptoed up the stairs.

Finally, he reached the fifth floor. He stood in the shadows and counted off the doors, trying to figure out which room the sniper was in. All the doors had been taken off their hinges, maybe used for firewood by the German soldiers, so he moved down the hallway, peeking into apartments.

The first apartment was vacant, and so was the second. Approaching the third, he smelled gunpowder and knew the sniper was in there. The building echoed with the sound of a rifle shot as the sniper fired again. Mahoney stood beside the doorway and peeked into the apartment. He saw the sniper

kneeling in front of a window, taking a clip of bullets out of
the pouch on his belt.

Mahoney stepped sideways into the doorway and simultaneously pulled the trigger of his carbine. It was an automatic, and the bullets spit out at the German, who jumped into
the air and spun around, howling wildly and dropping his
rifle, trying to cover all the holes in his body. He fell to the
floor.

"Was ist los!" shouted a German voice.

Mahoney realized suddenly that another German sniper
was in the building, too. Dashing into the room with the
German he'd just killed, Mahoney pressed his back to the
wall and pulled a hand grenade from his lapel.

"Hans?" asked a voice down the hall.

Mahoney pulled the pin from the grenade and realized that
two snipers must have been on that floor, and he cursed
himself because he should have been able to tell from the
muzzle blasts. But he'd made the mistake of thinking that
only one German was doing all the shooting. At night, from a
distance, both of the muzzle blasts looked as if they were
coming from the same place.

"Hans?" asked the wary voice again.

Mahoney heard footsteps in the hall; the other German was
coming to see what had happened. Pulling back his arm,
Mahoney tossed the grenade in the direction of the footsteps,
then pressed his back to the wall again.

The grenade exploded with a mighty roar, and the walls of
the building trembled. Mahoney jumped into the hallway and
saw the second German all over the walls and floor. His own
mother wouldn't have recognized him.

Mahoney returned to the room where he'd shot the first
sniper. The German lay sideways on the floor, his eyes wide
open and staring. He'd been alive one moment and dead the
next. It must have been quite a shock in that final split second
before his lights went out. *Not a bad way to go*, Mahoney
thought, kneeling beside the German and taking his gold
watch off his wrist. *I hope that when my time comes, I can go
as fast*.

He searched the German's pockets and found his wallet.
Opening it, he took out some German money and noticed a

photograph of a beautiful blonde woman. On the bottom was inscribed in German: To my darling Hans, from Frieda.

Mahoney looked at the dead German, who was no more than twenty years old. *Well*, Mahoney thought, *you sure got some good poontang in your short life*. He put the wallet back in the German's pocket and left the room. Descending the stairs, he left the building and moved quickly through the night, heading for Charlie Company so that he could report to Captain Anderson that the snipers in that building were out of action.

Mahoney's return was much quicker than his trip to the building. He was challenged by sentries, gave the correct countersign, and slid down a ditch, crossed some railroad tracks, and ascended the other side of the ditch, making his way to the railroad station that Captain Anderson was using as his command post for the night.

TWENTY-ONE

It was three o'clock in the morning in Metz's big railroad terminal. It was raining again, and the two battalions of shock troops were loading on to the freight and passenger cars hooked up behind the two locomotives. General Neubacher and Colonel Knoedler, accompanied by Lieutenant Stahmer and Col. Gunther Heiden, the latter designated as commander of the military force, strolled alongside the trains, looking at the men who would turn the tide of battle in Metz.

"They're young," said Heiden, a stern-looking man of fifty.

"But they're fine soldiers," Neubacher replied. "After all, enthusiasm is often better than experience in war."

"I suppose you're right," Heiden said, although he didn't agree with General Neubacher. Heiden had seen many enthusiastic soldiers slaughtered in the First World War and the one he presently was in and couldn't place any great faith in that factor alone.

Neubacher looked at Stahmer. "The locomotives are mechanically sound?"

"They could go all the way to Paris if they had to," Stahmer replied.

"Good man."

The young soldiers loaded into the cars, their uniforms clanking. They laughed and joked with each other, confident that they would win a great battle before the sun came up in the morning. All of them were officer candidates, and they understood von Clausewitz's main principles of war. In this particular battle, they would have the principles of mass, maneuver, economy of force, and surprise on their side, for they were concentrating two battalions on a very narrow section of the American line and the Americans had no idea that they were coming.

The officers strolled past the cars to the lead locomotive, from which the operating engineer looked down at them. Neubacher looked at his watch.

"Well, the time is rapidly approaching," he said. "I would like to wish all of you good luck."

"Thank you, sir," said Heiden and Stahmer.

They all saluted and shook hands.

"Once you start moving," Neubacher told them, "you'd better go at top speed because sooner or later the Americans will hear you coming. You don't want to give them time to get organized."

Heiden nodded. "We understand, sir."

Heiden and Stahmer climbed into the engine room of the locomotive, joining the three army engineers who were already there. General Neubacher gave the signal, and Stahmer told the engineers to move out.

The engineers turned cranks and pulled levers. Steam and sparks shot into the air from the chimney and exhaust valves of the gigantic engine. One of the engineers shoveled fire into the furnace, and Stahmer looked inside at the coals that glowed cherry red.

The wheels spun on the tracks, and the locomotive moved forward, pulling the cars behind it. Generals Neubacher and Knoedler stepped back and threw the Hitler salute as the locomotive passed by them. The soldiers in the cars approached the generals and saluted them back. It was a thrilling moment, their hearts welded together by their great common purpose. Spontaneously, they opened their mouths and sang one of their battle songs:

And so we march
and so we fight, fight, fight
for our Fuehrer
and for our Fatherland

Holding his arm in the air, Neubacher turned to Knoedler and said: "With fine young men like these, how can we fail?"

"Well," replied Knoedler, "one can always fail, but it would be awfully difficult with these soldiers."

The first train rattled and chattered as it passed the two generals, and then the second locomotive came close behind it, the engineer peering out the side of his cockpit and behind him the soldiers singing and holding their arms out in the Hitler salute.

The trains gathered speed and rolled out of the railroad yard. The generals watched them go, each wishing he could be part of the battle, too.

Neubacher lowered his arm and tried to shake some blood into it. "Well," he said to Knoedler, looking at the trains disappearing into the night and rain, "it's all in the hands of God now."

Mahoney opened his eyes in the darkness. He thought he'd been dreaming about the choo-choo of a locomotive, but now he was wide awake and still could hear it coming from the center of Metz, where the Germans were.

He sat up and shook his head. What the hell's going on here? Putting on his helmet, he stepped over sleeping bodies and made his way to the door of the railroad station, opening it up. He looked into the distance down the length of railroad track but couldn't see anything. Taking off his helmet, he scratched his head and wondered what was happening. If the Germans were trying to break out of the encirclement of Metz, they'd head east toward their country and toward France unless—

A terrifying thought entered Mahoney's brain. He slammed his helmet on to his head and ran back into the railroad station.

"Get up, everybody!" he yelled. "The krauts are coming!"

The men, who'd been sleeping soundly, jumped to their feet. "Where!" they asked. "What!"

"Get your weapons!" Mahoney shouted. "Put together the bazookas! Move your fucking asses!"

Captain Anderson buckled on his cartridge belt. "What's wrong, sergeant?"

"The Germans are coming, sir! Listen!"

A hush fell over the room. In the distance, the sound of the locomotive came through the rain.

"I can hear it!" said Captain Anderson.

"It's coming closer!" added Sergeant Tweed.

Mahoney turned to Captain Anderson. "I think you'd better call battalion and tell them the Germans are coming, sir!"

"But you don't know that," Anderson said, fearing to spread a false alarm.

"Well, something sure as hell is coming. Maybe you'd better alert them that a locomotive is headed this way."

"Yes, you're right, of course, Mahoney," Anderson replied. "That much we can say for sure."

"And we also can guess," Mahoney continued, "that those locomotives must be pulling something, like maybe troops or artillery, so you might mention that to battalion, too, sir."

"Right." Anderson turned to Private, First Class Drago. "Bring me the radio set."

"Yes, sir."

Drago brought Anderson the radio set as Mahoney tried to organize the men. "We've got to take up defensive positions fast!" Mahoney said. "All the bazookas should be ready to fire because we'll want to stop that fucking train!"

The men hooked together the two halves of the bazookas, and some of them checked the haversack that carried the bazooka shells. Anderson finally got through to battalion headquarters, and the men scurried around the train station, putting on their equipment and getting ready for a fight.

They could hear the sound of the locomotive much clearer in the distance now. It was coming closer, and they figured it would reach them in a matter of minutes.

The locomotives roared at top speed through the devastated city. In the cars, the young officers brandished their rifles and sang songs, their faces flushed with excitement. Everyone knew the importance of the mission. Everyone was ready to give his all in this great battle for the city of Metz.

In the leading locomotive, the engineers manipulated levers and studied dials, while one of them continued to shovel coal into the furnace. Lieutenant Stahmer leaned out the window, feeling the wind in his face and watching buildings and boulevards pass by. Even he, a devout coward, was becoming exhilarated by the speed of the train and the adventure that lay ahead. *What a brilliant idea this was*, he thought. *How can we fail?*

The train chugged around corners and down straight lengths of track. German soldiers on the ground took off their helmets and cheered them on. It was like a big party. Everyone was confident of success.

The train thundered through a tunnel, climbed a hill, and turned a corner; straight ahead were the American lines.

"Full speed ahead!" yelled Stahmer, his eyes ablaze.

The engineers turned the knobs and pulled levers all the way. Random bullets ricocheted off the locomotive and the railway cars as some American soldiers saw the train and took potshots at it.

Stahmer turned to Colonel Heiden. "We've taken them completely by surprise, sir! The battle is won!"

"Here they come," Mahoney said grimly, the bazooka resting on his shoulder.

Private Riggs was behind him, twisting the rocket wires to the terminal posts on the back of the bazooka. Charlie Company was lined up on both sides of the gully through which the train would pass. Each ridge line was twenty yards from the tracks, close enough to shoot Germans between the eyes.

The GIs saw the train coming at them, spewing sparks into the air. They didn't know yet that another train was behind the first one, carrying just as many troops. Captain Anderson had called battalion, and reinforcements were on the way, but Charlie Company would have to hold the Germans until the reinforcements arrived.

The train sped toward them, and Mahoney got up on one knee, pointing the bazooka downward. All of the eight bazookas in Charlie Company were aimed at the train, and the signal to fire would come from Mahoney. His first shot would tell them to begin. The train rushed toward him, sending billows of steam into the night.

Mahoney aimed at the leading locomotive, following it with the crosshairs of his bazooka. The locomotive pulled abreast of him, and he fired at pointblank range. The rocket whizzed out of his bazooka and flew toward the locomotive slowly enough so he could see it. It hit and exploded, sending streaks of red and orange in all directions. Farther down the line, the other bazookas were fired, and the GIs opened up with their rifles and machine guns. There were a series of explosions, but the train kept going. Riggs loaded another rocket into Mahoney's bazooka as Mahoney aimed at the lead locomotive again. Riggs tapped Mahoney's helmet, the signal that the rocket was ready, and Mahoney fired again.

This time he aimed low, and the rocket blew the drive mechanism and a wheel of the train to bits. Near Mahoney, a machine gunner raked the cab of the locomotive with bullets, and the train slowed down. Smoke and steam poured out of the hole caused by Mahoney's first rocket. But the train kept going, and after ten more yards it tripped the booby trap that Mahoney and Cranepool had set. The trap consisted of a stack of hand grenades activated by a wire, and they exploded with such force that they lifted the front of the locomotive three feet in the air. When the locomotive came down, it landed in the hole that the grenades had just made. The locomotive couldn't move forward, but the train still had momentum. Cars crashed into each other and jackknifed off the track. German soldiers screamed and tried to jump clear, but some of them couldn't get out of their cars and were trapped or crushed to death. Then the second locomotive crashed into the first train.

The men of Charlie Company fired at the Germans pouring out of the wreckage of the trains. The GIs realized that a great many German soldiers were down there, and Charlie Company was vastly outnumbered. Their only hope was that the Germans would be too confused to mount an attack and that by then reinforcements from battalion would arrive.

Mahoney's first rocket jolted the locomotive and caused Stahmer to fall, knocking his helmet off. The second rocket and subsequent grenade explosions sent Stahmer flying against an iron wall, splitting his head open. Blood poured from the crack in his hair, and you didn't have to be a doctor to know that he wouldn't live very long.

Colonel Heiden was knocked unconscious for only a few

seconds, and now he arose from the steam and smoke inside the cab of the locomotive, drawing his pistol. *The plan failed,* he thought. *We've been ambushed. But we're not finished yet.*

"Out of the cars!" he shouted. "Forward!" He jumped down from the cab as bullets whistled and ricocheted all around him. "Charge!" He ran back to rally his men, but three bullets from a BAR caught him in the shoulder and chest. He went flying against the undercarriage of an overturned railroad car, slid down it, and died in the mud and rain.

The young officer candidates jumped from windows and doors of their railroad cars. They'd been ambushed, and many had been killed, but the majority still were alive. They quickly grasped their situation and saw where the Americans were.

"Fix bayonets!" their officers and sergeants shouted. "Charge!"

The young men fastened their bayonets to the ends of their rifles and ran toward the flashes of light on the ridge line that ran beside the railroad tracks. They still were optimistic and thought that somehow they could turn the initial setback around. Shouting battle cries and firing from the hip, they rushed up the incline and hoped to overwhelm the Americans with the weight of their numbers and the intensity of their attack.

Mahoney saw the Germans charging toward him. He fired his carbine on automatic, but they kept coming, jumping over their dead comrades, shouting encouragement to each other, holding their rifles high. Like water that had been dammed, they rushed up the incline toward the GIs, who waited grimly for them.

Mahoney rose from the ground, planted his left foot behind him, and pointed his carbine and bayonet at the Germans. They came closer, howling and screaming, and enveloped the GIs. Rifles slammed against rifles, and bayonets plunged through uniforms into flesh. They tried to stab each other with their bayonets and bash each other's heads with their rifle butts.

Mahoney wished he had a rifle because a carbine was a puny weapon in hand-to-hand combat, but he made up for the lack with his considerable bodily strength and experience at close combat. A young German soldier, his eyes glittering with the excitement of battle, ran toward Mahoney and tried to impale him with his bayonet, but Mahoney sidestepped deftly and banged the German in the nose with his rifle butt. The German's eyes stopped glittering, and he fell to his knees, blood pouring from the mangled mess his nose had become. Mahoney snatched the rifle out of his hands, and now he was ready for serious warfare.

He kicked the German in the face, leaped over him, and landed in front of another young German with the face of an angel. The German shouted something and streaked his bayonet toward Mahoney's heart, but Mahoney put his full weight behind a parry, pushing the German's rifle and bayonet to the side. The German looked surprised, and Mahoney brought his rifle butt around, slamming it into the German's face. Blood squirted out the German's ears and nose, and Mahoney lunged forward with his bayonet, jamming it to the hilt into the German's stomach.

Mahoney charged the next German, who'd lost his helmet somewhere and had enormous ears.

Mahoney feinted with his bayonet, and the German raised his rifle to block the lunge that never came. Instead, Mahoney aimed lower and pushed his bayonet into the German's lower abdomen. The German howled in pain and dropped his rifle, trying to stanch the flow of blood with his hands, and Mahoney bashed him in the face, turning to the side to meet a German rushing toward him, but Mahoney couldn't get his guard up in time, and the German's bayonet cut into Mahoney's pectoral muscle before Mahoney could stop it.

Mahoney felt as though he'd been touched with a red-hot poker, and that made him mad. He took a step backward, parried another lunge from the German, and tried to stick the German himself, but the German got out of the way.

Mahoney and the German circled each other, feinting with their bayonets. Mahoney could see that this German was a sergeant like himself. He probably was an old hand at this sort of thing, and Mahoney realized he'd have his hands full this time. The German smiled faintly and appeared confident. His bayonet and the barrel of his rifle were covered with blood, which told Mahoney that the German had been having a good day so far.

The German hooted like a wild bull and charged forward, streaking his bayonet toward Mahoney's heart. Mahoney didn't dodge out of the way or step back. He met the thrust straight on and parried it with the trigger guard of his rifle. The German's bayonet missed Mahoney's left bicep by an inch, and the force of the German's attack brought him so close to Mahoney that their faces almost touched. Mahoney could smell the German's sour breath and see the stubble on his chin. He pushed the German, and the German pushed him back. They grappled, trying to trip each other and knock each other down. The German spit in Mahoney's eyes, trying to blind him, and Mahoney tried to kick the German in the balls, but the German managed to avoid the blow.

They struggled with each other, cursing and snarling. The German gritted his teeth, summoned all his strength, and pushed as hard as he could. Mahoney saw him coming and stepped to the side like a matador. The German stumbled over his own feet, stabbing at thin air, and Mahoney laughed as he thrust his bayonet into the German's kidney. The German screamed like a wild animal and turned around to face Mahoney. Terror was in the German's eyes because he realized he'd gambled and lost. Mahoney feinted with his bayonet, and the German feebly tried to block the blow. The German looked confused, and Mahoney shoved his bayonet into the German's throat.

A German shouted nearby, and pointed at Mahoney. He ran toward Mahoney with two of his comrades, evidently to avenge the death of the sergeant Mahoney had just killed. The battlefield was crowded, and Mahoney didn't want to shoot anybody from Charlie Company, but it was kill or be killed. He raised the German rifle to his shoulder and fired at the German on the left. The German tripped and fell, a bullet in his chest, and Mahoney brought the rifle down to eject the shell because German Mauser rifles were bolt-action designs and not automatic like the American rifles and carbines. But he couldn't eject the shell and fire again in time. The two Germans swarmed over him, trying to stab him with their bayonets. They were young men and appeared angry. They must have loved their sergeant, but Mahoney loved his life more.

He dodged and parried, feinted and lunged, trying to keep

the Germans off him while ejecting the shell and slamming a new one into the chamber. One of the Germans realized what he was doing and squeezed the trigger of his own rifle. But before it could fire, Mahoney shot him in the chest, then wheeled suddenly to the side and thrust his bayonet into the last German, whose expression of anger turned suddenly to fear. He parried Mahoney's attempt to kill him, but Mahoney pulled his bayonet back, swung his rifle butt around, and hammered the German in the jaw, knocking it loose from its hinges. The German dropped to the ground, and Mahoney stood over him, pushing his bayonet into the German's heart. The German went limp, and Mahoney stepped over him, feeling bloodthirsty and wild, looking for someone else to kill.

Cranepool had a hatchet that he'd taken from a dead engineer when they'd been thrown back across the Moselle near Pont-á-Mousson. He'd kept it in his pack for a time like this, and now he was swinging it with both hands, splitting German skulls and chopping Germans down like trees.

Cranepool had lost control of himself, but it was okay because he was in a war. His eyes gleamed like a madman as he crashed the hatchet into the neck of a German, nearly taking off his head. Blood gushed out like a fountain, hitting Cranepool in the face, but he licked his lips and spun like a dervish, whacking Germans in the arms and legs, splitting open their collarbones, and chopping their skulls in two like coconuts.

His normally placid all-American-boy features had become a mask of fury as he charged Germans and swung his hatchet at them. They fell back before the savagery of his attack, and he chased them, swinging his hatchet. Breathing like a horse who'd run a mile, he peered through the smoke and rain and saw a German officer calmly taking aim at him with a pistol.

"Yaaaahhhh!" Cranepool screamed, charging the officer, poising his hatchet to split his skull.

The officer didn't flinch as he slowly squeezed his trigger. The pistol barked, and Cranepool felt a hot slug rip into his stomach. He staggered but didn't fall. Blinking, unable to believe he'd been hit after three years of war, he told his feet to move forward and tried to raise his hatchet so he could smite the officer who'd shot him. His arm only went up halfway, and the German aimed carefully at him again.

"Yaaaahhhhh!" Cranepool yelled in defiance as blood oozed out of his stomach.

The German officer squeezed his trigger. A shot rang out, and the German officer twitched. His hand faltered and dropped slowly. He appeared not to know what had hit him. Another shot rang out, and the German officer dropped to his knees, his head bent over as if in prayer. Cranepool looked to the side and saw Captain Anderson, a smoking .45 in his hand. The German officer pitched forward on to his face, and Captain Anderson ran toward Cranepool.

"You all right, Corporal?"

"I'm hit in the stomach, sir," Cranepool said, his head spinning.

"You'd better lie down."

"You'd better watch out for that kraut with the bayonet, sir," Cranepool whispered.

Captain Anderson turned, and sure enough there was a German with a bayonet charging them. Anderson raised his .45 and drilled him through the gut. The German stumbled and fell to the ground, a small puncture in the front of his stomach, his kidneys and liver blown out of his back.

Cranepool realized he was lying on the ground. He didn't know how he'd got there. Captain Anderson kneeled over him.

"Medic!" yelled Captain Anderson. "I want a medic over here right now!"

Americans and Germans struggled all around them, and whenever a German got too close, Anderson shot him with his Colt .45. Then, out of the tumult of battle, Private Grossberger, his eyeglasses taped to his head, appeared with his bag of medicine, running in a wild zigzag, dodging bullets and bayonets. When he got close to Captain Anderson and Cranepool, he leaned back and slid toward them like Joe DiMaggio sliding into second base.

"Wow—it's Cranepool!" Grossberger said, opening his bag of medicine.

"He's been hit in the stomach," Anderson said.

Cranepool groaned and looked up at Grossberger, his eyes pleading for help. Grossberger took out a morphine ampule, broke the seal, and jabbed it through Cranepool's pants into his big thigh muscle.

"You'll be okay, Cranepool, old boy," Grossberger said, squeezing the morphine into Cranepool's body.

Cranepool didn't feel anything yet. "I'm bleeding," he mumbled.

Grossberger threw the ampule over his shoulder, took out a pocket knife, and cut open Cranepool's shirt so that he could see the wound. It was an ugly one but not bleeding too badly. Grossberger sprinkled on some blood coagulant, then placed a big gauze bandage over the wound, flinching as Captain Anderson fired his .45 at Germans nearby.

Captain Anderson ejected an empty clip and slammed a fresh one into the handle of his .45. The German soldiers were swarming all over his men, and he wondered where the reinforcements were. It seemed as though hours had passed since he'd called battalion.

It's like Custer's last stand, he thought, kneeling beside Grossberger and Cranepool, picking off any German who ventured too close.

Mahoney was surrounded by Germans trying to jab him with their bayonets. He twisted and dodged, banging them with his rifle butt, parrying their thrusts, and slicing open their bellies. He broke through the ring around him, spun around, and pulled his trigger, but nothing happened because he'd forgot to eject the last round he fired. *Fucking no-good kraut rifles*, he thought as two of the Germans charged him from the front and another attacked from his rear.

I can't keep holding them off, Mahoney thought, his arms growing weary. I'm going to die in this goddamn city that I never heard of before. He bashed one German in the face with his rifle butt and kicked another in the balls. The third German lunged with his bayonet, and Mahoney managed to deflect it downward, but the bayonet slashed open Mahoney's leg. The pain made Mahoney jump two feet in the air and holler at the top of his lungs. Angrier than ever, not caring whether he lived or died, he charged the German with such ferocity that the German had to backstep. Mahoney smashed the rifle out of the German's hands and pounded him in the face with his rifle butt. The German fell at his feet, and

Mahoney wanted to stomp his face into mush, but there were other Germans all around him, and he didn't have time.

He heard a commotion in the distance and at first didn't know what it was. He just kept fighting for his life as blood dripped out of the wound on his leg and flowed into his combat boots. Believing he was bleeding to death, he fought harder than ever, screaming and yelling at the Germans, daring them to come closer.

The commotion became louder and sounded like huge numbers of men rushing toward him with equipment rattling, shouting battle cries in English. It dawned on Mahoney that reinforcements finally were on the way. "Hooray!" he yelled. "We've got 'em now, boys!" He charged and drove his bayonet to the hilt into the chest of a young German officer candidate.

The Germans knew that American reinforcements were coming, but they were fanatical soldiers and refused to retreat. The Americans rolled over them, shooting and stabbing, outnumbering them five to one. The tide of battle turned suddenly, but the Germans wouldn't surrender. They stood and fought as best they could, but they didn't have a chance. In less than a half hour, the battle was over. Both sides of the railroad tracks were strewn with the bodies of Germans and Americans. The air was filled with moans and shouts of pain. Bodies writhed in pain, and the American medics worked as quickly as they could, first attending to their comrades and then trying to save the few Germans who were still alive.

As dawn broke on the horizon, Mahoney stood and leaned on the German rifle as a medic whom he didn't know bandaged his leg.

"You'll be okay, sarge," the medic said, wrapping the bandage around Mahoney's thigh. "You might have a little trouble walking around for a while, but that should be all."

Mahoney took out his package of Luckies and lit one up. He felt exhausted and was profoundly disgusted with the war. *I can't take much more of this,* he thought. *I'm going to get killed out here one of these days.*

Corporal Shackleton from the weapons platoon saw Mahoney and walked over toward him. "How're you doing, sarge?"

"How does it look like I'm doing?" Mahoney replied.

"Too bad about Cranepool, huh?"

Mahoney felt as if somebody had hit him over the head with a monkey wrench. "What about Cranepool!"

Shackleton took a step backward. "You didn't know?"

"Know what, you fucking asshole!"

"Cranepool got hit."

Mahoney felt himself becoming woozy.

The medic looked up at him. "You okay, sarge?"

"Yeah." Mahoney stared at Shackleton. "Cranepool got hit?"

"Right in the gut. He ain't dead, though. I think they evacuated him back to the dressing station."

"Jesus Christ," Mahoney said, wanting to fall down and close his eyes. "Good God."

"Captain Anderson was with him when he got hit. He can tell you what happened."

"Where's he at?"

Shackleton pointed. "Last time I saw him he was over thataway."

Mahoney slung his German rifle over his shoulder and limped in the direction Shackleton had indicated. He couldn't believe that Cranepool finally had been hit and was overcome by gloomy foreboding. Cranepool had been his good-luck charm throughout the war, and Mahoney thought he would live as long as Cranepool stayed alive, but now Cranepool had been wounded, and stomach wounds could be bad. *I'm not going to survive the war*, Mahoney thought. *I'm a dead duck*.

He trudged around medics treating wounded men and stepped over dead bodies. It was still raining, and Mahoney felt utterly desolate. He spotted Captain Anderson surrounded by a group of officers from battalion headquarters. Colonel Sloan, the battalion commander, was talking with Anderson.

"You've done a fine job here, captain," said "Rabbit" Sloan, so named because of his protruding two front teeth.

"Thank you, sir."

"If it hadn't been for you and your men, there might have been a German breakthrough."

"Actually, one of my sergeants was the first to be aware that the trains were coming."

"Which one was he?"

"Mahoney, sir."

"Master Sergeant Mahoney?"

"Yes, sir."

"Isn't he the one who used to be in the Rangers?"

"Yes, sir."

"By God, I think I see him over there." Colonel Sloan waved at Mahoney. "Come on over here, sergeant?"

"Yes, sir," Mahoney said, limping over.

"What happened to your leg?" Sloan asked.

"Don't remember," Mahoney replied, throwing a sloppy salute.

"You're bleeding from your chest, too."

"It's only a little cut, sir."

"Captain Anderson told me you sounded the alarm on these trains."

"That's right, sir." Mahoney looked at Captain Anderson. "Do you know what happened to Corporal Cranepool, sir?"

"He's on his way back to the battalion aid station," Anderson replied.

"He hurt bad?"

"Private Grossberger didn't think so. It was a stomach wound."

"Who's Corporal Cranepool?" Sloan asked.

"He was with Sergeant Mahoney in the Rangers, sir," Anderson replied.

"Sir," said Mahoney, "do you think I could go back to the aid station and see how he is? I could get my leg looked at while I'm there."

Everybody looked down at Mahoney's leg.

"You're losing a lot of blood, segeant," Colonel Sloan said.

"Yes, sir."

"Is that a German rifle you're carrying?"

"I think so, sir."

Sloan smiled. "You're not in the German Army now, are you, sergeant?"

"I don't think so, sir."

"Then maybe you'd better get an American weapon."

"Yes, sir."

Sloan looked at Anderson. "I think you can let him go

back to the battalion aid station. In fact, I think your whole company can go into reserve for a little while.''

Anderson smiled. ''I think the men would appreciate that, sir.''

Mahoney eased away from the group of officers, who resumed their discussion of the battle that had just taken place. He threw away his German rifle and picked up an M-1 that he saw lying on the ground. Slinging it over his shoulder, he began his journey back to the battalion aid station.

TWENTY-TWO

Colonel Knoedler hung up the telephone, his face drained of color. He took a deep breath, then walked to General Neubacher, who was standing at the map table. General Neubacher looked up.

"What is it, Knoedler?" he asked.

"Sir," said Knoedler, "the attack has failed."

Neubacher dropped the pencil in his hand. "Failed?"

"Yes, sir. Evidently, the Americans heard the train coming and had time to set up a road block. They stopped the train and apparently overwhelmed our assault troops."

Neubacher closed his eyes. "No," he whispered. "It can't be." He opened his eyes. "How did you come by this information?"

"An artillery observer in that sector saw what happened and filed a report."

"Then it must be true," Neubacher said.

"I'm afraid so, sir."

Neubacher didn't want to say it, but he knew that all was lost. His orders were to hold the city at all costs, but he knew that he couldn't hold it now. It was only a matter of time before the Americans crushed all resistance in front of them. When the battle reached its final stages, then he might withdraw. But he'd make the Americans pay for every inch of ground that they won.

"Do you have any new orders, sir?" Knoedler asked.

Neubacher squared his shoulder. "My orders remain the same. We will fight the Americans and throw them out of Metz."

"Yes, sir."

"I shall be in my quarters if you need me for anything."

"Yes, sir."

Neubacher left the conference room and walked down the corridor to his quarters, thinking of the young men who'd gone off in the trains. They'd been so enthusiastic, singing their song. Neubacher almost could hear their voices:

> And so we march
> and so we fight, fight fight
> for our Fuehrer
> and for our Fatherland

"Ach, what a waste," Neubacher muttered as he opened the door to his room.

Cranepool lay on the floor of the battalion aid station, smoking a cigarette. He was still dizzy from the morphine shot and saw little blinking lights on the ceiling. Sometimes he heard music and the sound of a breeze in willow trees. He was barely aware of the ache in his stomach and thought the morphine was awfully nice stuff.

His only problem was that he felt lonely on the floor with men he'd never seen before in his life, and he was concerned that after he was operated on, they'd send him back to some other unit than Charlie Company. He knew that the army did things like that because replacements often showed up in Charlie Company who'd previously been in other units.

He raised his head a few inches off the floor and looked around the room. It was large, evidently a public room of some kind, and nurses and orderlies were going from man to man, checking wounds, changing bandages, giving shots. He was in the group that would be going into the operating room soon. Another group was recovering from operations. A third group was dead or dying.

Cranepool thought he saw Mahoney limp through a door, but Cranepool figured the morphine was making him see things. Mahoney looked around the room, and Cranepool raised his hand on the chance that maybe it really was Mahoney over there. The apparition saw his hand and grinned, walking toward him, limping up the aisle.

"How's it going, kiddo?" Mahoney asked, kneeling down beside Cranepool. "How're the bastards treating you?"

"Are you for real?" Cranepool asked dizzily.

"Are you crazy? Of course I'm for real."

"Good," Cranepool said, "because I wasn't sure."

"You must be shot full of dope up to your eyeballs,"
Mahoney said. "How're you doing otherwise?"

"Pretty good. They're gonna operate on me in a little
while."

"What happened to you?"

"A German shot me with his Luger."

"You'd better be thankful that the Germans don't have
forty-fives."

"There wouldn't be much left of me if they had forty-
fives."

Mahoney turned around and saw the hindquarters of a
nurse bending over one of the soldiers. "Holy shit—looka
there. She's taking my picture."

Cranepool reached up and touched Mahoney's sleeve.
"Sarge, what if they don't send me back to Charlie Company?"

"Come back, anyway. That's what I did."

"But they might say I'm AWOL."

"Fuck 'em."

"You got some pull with General Donovan, haven't you,
sarge? I mean, you're the division heavyweight champ, right?"

"Yeah."

"Will you talk to General Donovan for me if I don't get
transferred back to Charlie Company?"

"Sure thing, kid. I'll tell him that if you don't come back
to Charlie Company, I won't go in the ring for him anymore.
He'll get the message."

Cranepool smiled. "I appreciate that, sarge."

"Don't mention it, kid."

The nurse, a lanky redhead with freckles, continued examining soldiers and soon came close to Mahoney.

"Hey, nurse," Mahoney said, "I got this terrible pain
between my legs. Would you look at it for me?"

She glanced at him disapprovingly.

"What are you doing here?" she asked. "You look all
right to me."

Mahoney stood up and pointed to his leg. His pants were
torn, and the bloody bandage was clearly visible. "I'm
supposed to get this sewed up, ma'am."

She looked at his chest. "You're wounded there, too, aren't you?"

"That one's stopped bleeding, I think."

She pointed to a door on the other side of the room. "Go in there and take your pants off. I'll be right in, and I'll take care of you."

Mahoney made a face of mock embarrassment. "Take my pants off? Why, ma'am, what in the world are you going to do to me?"

"I don't have time for your foolishness," she said curtly. "Do as I say."

"Yes, ma'am." Mahoney slapped Cranepool on the shoulder. "Take it easy, kiddo, and don't worry about a thing. Let old Sergeant Mahoney do the worrying, okay?"

"Hup, sarge."

Mahoney stood and walked across the room, dragging his bad leg behind him. He opened the door the nurse had indicated and saw a chair, a long, narrow table, and cabinets filled with medicine. He leaned his rifle against the wall and sat on the chair, taking out a cigarette and lighting it up. The thick walls of the building muffled the sounds of fighting in the distance, and he felt as if he'd suddenly stepped out of the war. Closing his eyes, he thought of Cranepool. When he'd met the kid two years ago, Cranepool had been like an angel. He didn't drink, smoke, or screw girls. When they went into battle, bullets would fly around, and everybody would get hit, but not Cranepool. Then, gradually, Cranepool started drinking, smoking and chasing whores. Now he was as corrupted by the war as the rest of them; finally, this morning, he'd been hit. It was as if Cranepool's virtue had been an invisible shield that protected him from harm, but now that his virtue was gone, he had become vulnerable like any other soldier.

The nurse walked into the room. "I thought I told you to take off your pants," she snapped.

"Take it easy on me, nursie," Mahoney said. "I'm just a poor old soldier boy."

"Don't give me any of your crap," she said, looking sternly at him. "Take off your pants and lay on that table before I call the MPs."

Mahoney winked. "If I take off my pants, will you take off yours?"

"Don't be funny."

"I'm not trying to be funny."

"Listen here," she said, "I've got a whole building full of wounded soldiers, and I don't have time for your nonsense. Now take your pants off and lay on that table or else get the hell out of here."

"Yes, ma'am," Mahoney said, unbuckling his cartridge belt. "I can see that you don't take any guff from us soldiers, and there's no reason on earth why you should." He unbuttoned his pants and pushed them down to his ankles. "Do you mind if I don't take them off all the way, nurse, so's I don't have to take off my combat boots, too?"

"You don't have to take them off all the way," she said, working at one of the cabinets.

Mahoney shuffled across the room and lay on the table. She picked up his shirt and looked at the cut, deciding it might need a few stitches, too. Then she turned to the bloody bandage on his hairy leg. She couldn't help noticing his oversized dong.

"I'll have to give you a needle to numb your leg," she said.

"Just don't stab it in the wrong place," he replied.

She smiled in spite of herself, jabbed in the needle, withdrew it, and then untied the bandage. Mahoney looked down and saw a four-inch gash on his thigh. The nurse turned her back to Mahoney and rattled around at the cabinet, while Mahoney's leg became numb. Then she turned around and daubed his wound with a wet bandage, clearing away the clotted blood.

Mahoney couldn't feel much and looked up at the nurse's face. Back in New York, he wouldn't have looked at her twice, but here in Metz she looked awfully good to him. He imagined her wrapping her long legs around him as he humped her and thought of how nice it would be if he could caress her small breasts. He began to get an erection.

"Feeling a little frisky, are we, sergeant?" she asked.

"I'm afraid so, ma'am. You couldn't help me out, could you?"

She pulled back her arm and whacked his erection with the blade of her hand. It collapsed like a tree that had just been chopped down in a forest.

"That better, sergeant?" she asked, reaching for her needle and thread.

"You're a heartless woman," Mahoney replied, his eyes squinched shut in pain.

Adolf Hitler paced back and forth behind his desk, his hands clasped behind his back. General Jodl sat on a chair in front of the desk, watching his *Fuehrer* anxiously. Jodl just had delivered a communiqué to the *Fuehrer* concerning Metz. General Neubacher reported that he didn't think he could hold out much longer.

Suddenly, Hitler stopped and looked at Jodl. "There is only one thing to do," he said solemnly. "You will relieve Neubacher of command."

"Yes, *mein Fuehrer*," Jodl replied, writing on his note pad. "Who shall I replace him with?"

"Who do you suggest?"

"I don't know. I'll have to confer with General Balck."

"And General Balck will have to confer with his chief of staff, who will have to confer with someone else, and this whole mess will drag on." Hitler drew his eyebrows together. "The problem with this army is that there are too many conferences and not enough hard fighting. I want the decision to be made *right now!*"

"Well," replied Jodl, groping in the recesses of his mind, "perhaps we can replace Neubacher with his chief of staff."

"What's his name?"

"Knoedler."

"Never heard of him. He's probably infected with the same defeatism that has incapacitated General Neubacher. I should put them both before firing squads for failure to do their duty.

"But, my *Fuehrer*, the garrison at Metz is outnumbered, and they have no air cover. What can the generals do?"

"More than they're doing." Hitler made a fist and shook it in the air. "What we need at times like this is unshakable fanaticism. There is an SS commandant in Metz, isn't there?"

"I imagine so, *mein Feuhrer*," Jodl said. "That's not my department, and I can't say for sure."

"Then tell Himmler I want to see him immediately. He'll know."

Jodl rose from his chair. "Yes, *mein Feuhrer.*"

It was midmorning, and Mahoney walked through the streets of Metz on his way back to Charlie Company. He passed devastated buildings and piles of rubble while tanks and jeeps rolled by on their way to the front. The main battle was taking place in the center of Metz now, and it was only a matter of time before the city fell. Soldiers at the battalion aid station speculated that the end would come in three or four days at the most.

Mahoney was in a good mood, and he whistled a song as he moved along. The nurse had sewn up his leg and chest, and he hurt less than when he'd shown up at the aid station at dawn. They'd given him a good hot breakfast and a new pair of pants to replace the ones that had been torn by the German bayonet. The rain had stopped, although it looked as though it might start up again at any moment.

He was headed toward the part of the city where Charlie Company had been placed in reserve. He'd never been in that part of the city before, but he figured that if he continued in its general direction, he'd find Captain Anderson and the boys eventually. There was no reason to hurry, anyway. He might as well enjoy his freedom while he had the chance.

He came to an intersection and saw a narrow, winding street lined with trees denuded of branches. Many of the buildings on the street were still standing, and it reminded Mahoney somewhat of Greenwich Village in New York, where he used to go before the war and screw girls who claimed to be artists. Nostalgia swept over him, and he thought he'd stroll down the street since it was on the way to Charlie Company.

He turned the corner and walked down the street. The glass was blown out of nearly all the windows, and some of the buildings were little more than façades, but Mahoney felt removed from the war, as if he were strolling through a street in Greenwich Village, looking for a good bar and a crazy girl who wore a beret and had paint stains on her fingers. They liked to go to bed with guys like him, he'd discovered. It made them feel as if they were in the real world for a change.

He stopped beside a lamppost broken in half and lit a Lucky. Dropping his lighter into his pocket, he inhaled and looked up at the building in front of him. To his astonishment, a blonde girl was in the window. He blinked his eyes because he couldn't believe she was there, and she winked at him, crooking her finger.

Are the whores here already? Mahoney asked himself, heading toward the stoop of the building. It was a three-story residence made of brick and evidently had been quite nice at one time. He climbed the stoop and unslung his rifle just in case it was a trap. Entering the window, he walked through a door to the room the girl had been in, but she wasn't there. Looking around, he saw another door, and through it, a few rooms away, was the blonde girl. What an incredible stroke of luck, he thought. That nurse got my dick hard, and now I'll stick it into this blonde number.

He moved toward her, and she giggled, turning and running away. So she wants me to chase her, Mahoney thought with a grin. She wants to play little games. He followed her through the apartment, thinking of what the blonde would look like without any clothes on. She looked quite nice from the distance—a tall, cool drink of water.

He came to a door and saw a flight of stairs leading to the cellar. *What the hell's going on here?* Mahoney thought. He looked down the stairs and saw her leaning seductively against the wall below.

"Come up here," he told her in German.

"No, you come down here," she replied, turning and running away.

Mahoney tromped down the stairs, wondering where she'd gone. The cellar smelled damp and musty, and he saw an empty coal bin. The two eyes of a cat glowed evilly as they looked at Mahoney from a corner.

Mahoney moved in the direction the blonde had gone when suddenly a new smell assailed his nostrils. It was sweet and flowery, her perfume. He stopped dead in his tracks when he realized that it was the same perfume he'd smelled on

Kubiak's corpse in the battalion dressing station several days ago. *Oh-oh*, Mahoney thought.

He sidestepped into the darkness and took a hand grenade out of his field-jacket pocket. Yanking the pin, he clasped the arming lever tightly and placed his hand and the grenade back into his pocket.

"Where are you?" the girl asked in German.

"Over here," Mahoney replied, stepping out of the shadows.

He walked cautiously through the cellar, listening for unusual sounds. He saw the girl standing in a room, unbuttoning her blouse. Holding the grenade tightly, he entered the room and saw some blankets on the floor beside the blonde. An open door was on the other side of the room. Mahoney turned loose the lever of the hand grenade in his pocket, arming it.

"Why don't you put down your rifle?" the girl said, opening her blouse and revealing a pink brassiere.

Mahoney pulled the grenade out of his pocket and chucked it through the open door. The girl screamed, and Mahoney dropped to his stomach. The grenade exploded thunderously, and a hurricane of dust blew into the room. Mahoney jumped to his feet, and ran toward the door, clicking the safety off his rifle. Charging into the next room, he looked around quickly and saw German SS men lying everywhere, bleeding and mutilated, one of them decapitated. Another, missing a leg, tried to get up. Mahoney shot him through the head, then retreated back to the room where the blonde had been.

She was gone. He looked through the other door and saw her running toward the stairs. He dropped to one knee, brought his rifle butt against his shoulder, aimed for the center of her back, and squeezed the trigger. She danced in his sights, her arms flailing the air, and the M-1 fired. The impact of the bullet lifted her off the floor and sent her flying through the air. She landed on her stomach, and Mahoney ran toward her.

She tried feebly to crawl to the stairs. The back of her blouse was soaked with blood. Mahoney looked down at her and thought of Butsko and Kubiak lying dead in the aid station. He inserted his foot underneath her and kicked her over on to her back, then aimed his M-1 at her face.

Blood leaked out the corner of her mouth, and she held up her hand. ''No,'' she begged, ''please.''

''This is for Butsko and Kubiak,'' Mahoney said, and pulled the trigger.

TWENTY-EIGHT

TWENTY-THREE

The phone rang and Col. Anton Meier of the SS picked it up. "Yes?"

"This is Heinrich Himmler," said the voice on the other end, and it sounded very far away.

Meier shot to his feet and stood at attention. "My *Reichsfuehrer*," Meier stuttered, "this is such an honor. I hardly know—"

Himmler interrupted with his cold, metallic voice. "How are you today, Colonel Meier?" Himmler asked.

"How am I?" Meier replied. "Why, I'm fine, I'm very fine, and I—"

Himmler interrupted him again. "The *Fuehrer* would like to talk with you."

"Well, I—ah—" Meier was at a loss for words. He'd never spoken with the *Fuehrer* in his life, although he'd attended many of his speeches, sitting at the backs of auditoriums or way up in the balconies.

The familiar, hypnotic voice of Adolf Hitler came on the wire. "Good day to you, Colonel Meier."

Meier realized he'd better pull himself together *right now*. "Good day to you, my *Fuehrer*."

"I am told that you are a true National Socialist and that you will do anything for your country. Is that true, Meier?"

"Most assuredly it is true, my *Fuehrer*."

"I have an important task for you, Meier. I have selected you for it because I know you will have the zeal to carry it out. I hereby appoint you commander in chief of the garrison of Metz, and furthermore, from this moment forward, you will be a brigadier general."

Meier was speechless. All he could do was make some weird guttural sounds.

"Are you there, Meier?"

"Yes, my *Fuehrer.*"

"I thought that perhaps we'd been cut off."

"No, my *Fuehrer.* I was merely astounded by what you said."

"Listen to me carefully, General Meier," Hitler said. "A crucial battle is being waged in Metz even as we speak. It is imperative that Metz be held for as long as possible. Your orders are to defend Metz to the last man. Is that clear?"

"Yes, my *Fuehrer.*"

"And you are to use whatever means are at your disposal to do so. Do you understand?"

Meier didn't dare to mention the Zyklon B on the telephone, so he said: "Do I understand you to mean, my *Fuehrer,* that I may use whatever weapons I have here to stop the Americans?"

"That is exactly what I mean," Hitler replied. "I don't care if you have to level Metz to the ground. Just hold on there for as long as possible. You are not to surrender or retreat under any circumstances. Is that clear?"

"Yes, my *Fuehrer.*"

"I have complete confidence in you, General Meier. I'm sure that as a result of your efforts Metz will always represent a shining moment in the history of the Reich."

"Thank you, my *Fuehrer.*"

"Do you have any questions?"

"None whatever, my *Fuehrer.*"

"Do your duty, General Meier, and bear in mind that I am always with you in spirit."

"Yes, my *Fuehrer.*"

The connection went dead in Meier's ear. Meier stood and turned around, looking at the photograph of Adolf Hitler hanging on his wall. Hitler was giving a speech, holding his fist next to his heart. The energy of Adolf Hitler seemed to flow from the photograph into the being of General Meier.

"I will stop the Americans," Meier said to the photograph, "even if it costs my life."

General Neubacher went pale as he read the telegram from Rastenberg.

"What is it?" asked Colonel Knoedler, standing beside the map table.

"I've been relieved of command," Neubacher said in a voice so soft it was almost a whisper.

"What!"

Neubacher held out the telegram. Knoedler took it and read quickly. He turned pale, too, and threw the telegram on the map table. The conference room became silent, as the younger officers looked at the two generals in amazement.

"I don't believe it," Knoedler said.

"I do," Neubacher replied. "I think we should know by now that we can expect anything from those maniacs in Rastenburg."

The door was flung open, and Meier marched into the conference room, followed by a retinue of SS officers.

"What maniacs in Rastenburg?" he asked imperiously.

"What are you talking about?" Neubacher replied.

"Didn't you just say something about maniacs in Rastenburg?"

"No."

"I thought you did."

"You thought wrong."

"I see," Meier said, looking contemptuously at the army officers in the room. The insignia of a general in the SS already had been sewn to his collar. "I believe I know very well what you said, but there's no point in arguing the issue now. You have received word of my appointment from headquarters?"

"I have."

"Good. How soon can you clear out of here?"

"Immediately."

"Excellent. I shall notify the troops that they have a new commander in chief, one who will prosecute this war more vigorously than has been done in the past by certain people whose names I won't mention."

Without a word, Neubacher and his officers filed out of the conference room. Neubacher felt relieved; his ordeal was over. "Well, gentlemen," he said in the corridor, "you now have a new commander. I suggest you return to your quarters and await his orders. Colonel Knoedler, may I have a word with you?"

The young officers marched off to the bachelor officers' quarters, and Neubacher hoped they'd have sense enough to try and surrender to the Americans. Knoedler drew close to him.

"Come to my office," Neubacher told him. "I must speak with you alone."

They walked down the corridor to Neubacher's office, entered, and closed the door behind him. Neubacher bolted the door, then turned and faced Knoedler.

"I have a terrible premonition," Neubacher said. "I'm afraid that idiot will use his Zyklon B."

Knoedler took a step backward. "That's true!" he said. "I'd almost forgotten about that stuff!"

"I haven't. Meier is a madman, and he just might set it loose."

"How can we stop him?"

"You and I can't stop him. We can't take on the SS detachment in this city by ourselves."

"Perhaps we can rally the soldiers behind us."

"Extremely doubtful. They'll follow their orders and do their duty as always. That is the great virtue of the German soldier, but unfortunately it's not much of a virtue right now."

Knoedler sat on a chair and looked wilted. "What can we do?"

Neubacher paced the floor. "There's only one thing. We must tell the Americans."

"Tell the Americans!"

"What else? They're the only ones who could take action."

Knoedler shook his head. "But how can we tell the Americans"

"We'll simply go to them and tell them."

"But how can we get through their lines?"

"I don't know, but we'll have to try," Neubacher said. "If Meier uses poison gas here in Metz, the Americans may retaliate by using it on German cities. Also, if he uses the gas here, he'll probably kill as many German soldiers as Americans."

"He's crazy," Knoedler said.

"Well, we always knew that," Neubacher replied. "What we didn't know was that one day he'd be placed in charge."

"What a catastrophe," Knoedler moaned.

"Perhaps we can stop it," Neubacher replied, sitting in the chair behind his desk. "Here's my plan."

That night, under a fierce American artillery bombardment, General Neubacher, dressed in the uniform of a private in the Wehrmacht, made his way toward the American lines. He carried a Mauser rifle and a long bayonet and wore his helmet low over his eyes so that no one would recognize him. He knew that if he was discovered, he'd be put before a firing squad and shot, if he was lucky.

He also knew that in another part of the city, Colonel Knoedler was similarly dressed and also trying to surrender to the Americans. They hoped that one of them would get through to warn the Americans. Otherwise, Neubacher shuddered to think of what might happen if the gas was unleashed. People for miles around might be killed, and if the Americans decided to use poison gas themselves, it would be terrible for Germany, for the Americans had control of the air and could bomb German cities at will. Neubacher's wife and two daughters lived in Stuttgart, and he didn't want them to die from poison gas. The ordinary American bombing campaign was enough.

Neubacher made his way through the streets of the central city to the front lines. He passed artillery emplacements and columns of battle-weary soldiers. How strange and horrible it was to see the war from the viewpoint of the foot soldier, all alone and vulnerable to death at any moment. Not even when Neubacher was a young captain in the First World War had he known what this was like.

He heard a fierce battle taking place straight ahead and tried to get around it. Moving parallel to the front line, walking down streets cluttered with the debris of destroyed buildings, he thought after a while that he had passed the scene of the confrontation. He took a deep breath and passed between two buildings, heading directly toward the American lines.

"Halt, who goes there!" shouted a German soldier behind the house.

"Private Kreegar," answered Neubacher.

"Advance and give the countersign."

Neubacher advanced and said the password.

"Where are you going?" asked the soldier, a corporal who was looking Neubacher over suspiciously. He'd never seen a private this old in his military career.

"I've been ordered to scout the American lines straight ahead," Neubacher said.

The corporal became more suspicious when he heard Neubacher's educated Prussian accent and wondered whether Neubacher was a spy. "I think you'd better wait here a moment while I check with the sergeant of the guard."

"What for?" Neubacher asked.

"To make sure you're who you say you are."

Neubacher may have been old, but he still had a lot of strength and energy. Lunging forward, he pushed the corporal with both hands, knocking him backward. The corporal tripped and fell, and Neubacher ran into the night, heading toward the American lines.

"Sergeant of the guard!" the corporal yelled, getting up. "Sergeant of the guard!"

He raised his rifle to his shoulder and took aim at the figure disappearing into the darkness. He fired a shot, and the figure could be seen no more. *Did I get him?* the corporal wondered.

He thought he'd better make sure, although he didn't feel like venturing out into no man's land. Carefully, holding his rifle ready, he stepped over the bricks and chunks of plaster, heading toward the spot where he'd last seen the soldier who'd called himself Private Kreegar. He heard running footsteps behind him and saw the sergeant of the guard with a few privates.

"What's going on here!" said the sergeant of the guard, catching up with him.

"Somebody dressed as a German soldier tried to run to the American lines, but I think I shot him."

The group of German soldiers spread out and progressed into no man's land, searching the rubble for a sign of the soldier the corporal had shot at.

"There he is!" shouted one of the privates, pointing ahead of him.

They all ran forward and saw the soldier lying on his stomach in a puddle of mud. The sergeant of the guard grabbed his shoulder and pushed him on to his back.

"Is this the man you shot, corporal?" he asked.

The corporal looked at the face of the old soldier on the ground. The soldier's eyes were closed, and blood trickled out of his open mouth. "That's the one, sergeant."

"Good work." The sergeant took a closer look at the dead soldier. "You men pick him up and carry him back. I'm sure somebody from Intelligence will want to come and have a look at him."

Colonel Knoedler, also disguised as a private, crept along the track of the same railway line that had carried two battalions of soldiers to their deaths in the attack several days ago. He hid in the darkness provided by one of the ridges that lined the track and put his feet down carefully every time, for he had done a lot of hunting during his life and knew how to move silently.

He'd figured that the railroad tracks wouldn't be too closely watched anymore because American bombers had destroyed the railroad yard and much of this track the day after the attack. There would be soldiers from both armies in the vicinity, but he doubted whether anybody would be down in the gully where the track was, and so far he'd been right.

Ahead, on both sides of the track, he heard gunfire. He moved toward it apprehensively, hoping he could get through, and wondering how General Neubacher was making out. The gunfire was sporadic, and he was glad because it meant no great battle was being fought in the vicinity.

He continued to walk silently in the shadows of the ditch, listening for signs of danger, knowing that he'd be in serious trouble if a German sentry caught him. He'd heard stories of what Hitler had done to the generals who'd been involved in the bomb plot of July 20: he'd had them hung on meat hooks, where they died slowly, twisting in the wind. He could expect the same kind of treatment if he, a German general, were found trying to surrender to the Americans.

Soon he became aware that shots were being fired behind him and in front of him, the indication that he was in no man's land. Now he moved more slowly and carefully than ever, as pinpricks of perspiration covered his forehead. He was afraid to breathe too loudly for fear of being heard.

The next two hundred yards were the hardest of his life. He

bit his lower lip and placed his feet down gently, hunching low in the shadows, hoping no one would see him. Sometimes, hearing a sound, he'd freeze for several minutes until he was certain it was safe to move again.

Finally, all the shooting was behind him, and he realized that he was inside the American lines. Now he had to hope that an American soldier wouldn't shoot him on sight in his German uniform. He took a white handkerchief out of his back pocket and climbed the side of the ditch, hoping for the best. He wished he could have worn civilian clothes underneath his uniform, but there had been no civilian clothes available for him.

At the top of the ditch, he saw a nightscape of ruined buildings and shell craters. Metz had been a beautiful city once, but now it was a big junkyard. Knoedler noted the change without suffering much remorse. He was a professional soldier and knew that destruction follows in the wake of an army.

"Halt!"

Knoedler stopped cold and looked ahead of him but could see nothing. Trying to smile, he waved his white handkerchief in the air.

"Who goes there!" said a voice in English.

Knoedler spoke some English, and said in his thick German accent: "I am a German colonel and I wish to surrender!"

"Don't move, you cocksucker!"

Knoedler didn't move, and two American soldiers materialized out of the night in front of him. One was tall and the other short, and they both were filthy, bearded, and bedraggled. They pointed their rifles at Knoedler and stepped closer, their faces expressing extreme suspicion.

"Watch him," said the tall soldier. "If he moves, drill him."

The tall soldier checked Knoedler for weapons but couldn't find anything. Knoedler still held his hands in the air, trying to smile.

"I am a German colonel, and I wish to speak with your commanding officer about something important," Knoedler said in a thick German accent.

The American soldiers looked at each other.

"He don't look like no colonel to me," said the tall one.

"But why would he say he was if he wasn't?" replied the short soldier.

Knoedler cleared his throat. "I disguised myself as a private soldier so I could slip through the lines more easily."

"I think he's lying," said the tall one.

"Maybe he's not, Joe."

"Why would a German officer come through our lines? I think we ought to shoot the fucker where he stands."

"Come on, Joe," said the short soldier. "Don't be so crazy all your life. Let's bring him to Captain Bryans. He'll know what to do."

The tall soldier thought that maybe if he went to headquarters, he could get a hot cup of coffee.

"Okay," he said. "We'll take the fucker back." He looked at Knoedler. "You'd better not try anything funny, kraut, or I'll put a hole in your head."

TWENTY-FOUR

Mahoney felt a hand on his shoulder and came up out of a deep sleep, lunging at the throat of the person who'd touched him.

Private, First Class Drago pulled back quickly. "Jesus, sarge, whenever I have to wake you up, I take my life in my hands."

Mahoney yawned and looked at Drago through half-closed eyes. The rest of the first platoon was sprawled out around him, snoring or grumbling in their sleep. They were in the cellar of a bombed-out building not far from the front.

"What do you want this time?" Mahoney asked.

"Captain Anderson wants to speak to you right away."

"What's up?"

"I don't know, but it's something big. They want you at division."

"Division?"

"Yeah. We got a call from division, and after it was over, Captain Anderson said to get you on the double."

"Holy fuck, I can't even get a night's sleep!" Mahoney complained, reaching for his pack of Luckys.

"Come on, sarge. Captain Anderson is waiting for you."

Mahoney followed Drago out of the cellar, wondering what they wanted from him now. He limped slightly, for his wound was still healing, and they stumbled over wreckage to the building where Captain Anderson had set up his headquarters. A jeep with division markings was parked near the door to the building, and in the cellar, Captain Anderson sat behind his field desk, his helmet off and his reddish-blond hair tousled. Not far away, on a wooden folding chair, sat a soldier who Mahoney figured to be the driver of the jeep.

"What's up, sir?" Mahoney said, not bothering to salute.

"They want you at division," Captain Anderson said.

"What for?"

"Something special. They'll tell you when you get there."

Mahoney groaned because he knew that whenever they wanted him for something special, it usually meant risking his life more than usual. "Aw shit," he said.

"You'd better get going," Anderson told him. "Private Atkinson here has his jeep outside."

Mahoney followed Atkinson out the door, and Atkinson got behind the wheel of the jeep. Mahoney sat beside him, and Atkinson drove away.

It was a rocky, bumpy ride because all the streets were covered with debris. Mahoney puffed his cigarette and turtled his head into his field-jacket collar, shivering. Every night was a little colder, and soon winter would arrive with all its attendant miseries. It wasn't easy to fight when your hands and feet are numb and you can't even feel your trigger. "Aw fuck," Mahoney mumbled, wondering what it would be like to be a civilian again. The vision was almost beyond the capacity of his imagination. He'd been in the army so long he felt as if he'd been born in the supply room and issued out to the first company commander who walked by.

The jeep stopped in front of division headquarters, an old courthouse some distance back from the front lines.

"Follow me, sarge," Atkinson said.

Mahoney did so and soon came to an office where two other soldiers were sitting on chairs.

"Wait here," Atkinson told Mahoney. "Somebody will come for you pretty soon."

Atkinson left the room, and Mahoney sat on a chair. The two other soldiers looked at him, and he looked back. Nobody said anything; they all were too tired. They leaned their heads against the wall and closed their eyes. A few minutes later, another soldier joined them. After a while, a major entered the room and told everybody to follow him.

The four tired soldiers dragged their asses down the corridor and entered the office of General Donovan, who sat behind his desk looking grumpy. He had a potbelly and a deeply lined face with a pug nose. A few other officers were present, and Mahoney was surprised to see an elderly man in the uniform of a German SS man.

"Have a seat, men," said General Donovan.

The soldiers sat down. *Here it comes*, Mahoney thought.

"You've all been selected for an extremely important mission," Donovan said.

No shit, Mahoney thought.

"You don't have to go on the mission if you don't want to because it's going to be very dangerous. Let's not make any bones about that. But I hope you will because you're the only ones who can bring it off."

What a crock of shit, Mahoney thought.

Donovan stood and pointed to a city map hanging on the wall behind his desk. "Here," he said, "in Gestapo head-quarters, there is a vast quantity of poison gas called Zyklon B. We believe that the new German commandant of Metz will use this gas unless he's stopped, and the only way to stop him will be to kill him. If he cannot be stopped, there is every reason to believe that he'll unleash the gas, and it might very well kill everybody in the city, German and American alike. You men have been chosen to stop him. Each of you has been on special missions before behind the enemy lines, and each of you speaks German fluently. You will wear uniforms of the SS, infiltrate the German position, find the new German commandant, and kill him. Then you will return here. Any questions so far?"

One of the soldiers raised his hand to shoulder level. "How do we know that this information is true."

"Because we have received it from a very high source. Gentlemen, may I present Colonel Alfred Knoedler, the former chief of staff of the Metz garrison."

Colonel Knoedler smiled faintly, and the American soldiers stared at him because they'd never seen a German general this close before.

Mahoney raised his hand. "How do we know he's telling the truth?"

"Why," asked Donovan, "would he risk his life to tell a lie?"

Mahoney ran that one through his mind. He couldn't think of any good reason unless he didn't like the new commandant and wanted him knocked off, but surely there'd be a better way than coming over to the American and telling that story. It's a wonder he wasn't killed when he tried to get through our lines, Mahoney thought.

"Any other questions?" General Donovan asked.

No one said anything.

"Good," said Donovan. "You'll have to act fast because we're pressing in on the center of the city, and the Germans can't hold out much longer. This new German commandant may set off the gas at any time. He must be stopped."

Mahoney raised his hand. Donovan looked annoyed. "Yes?"

"Sorry to interrupt you, sir, but another question just came to my mind. If we kill this kraut commandant, how do we know that the next kraut commandant won't do the same thing?"

"Because Colonel Knoedler here has assured me that the present commandant is the only man in Metz who would do such a horrendous thing. The commandant, whose name is Meier, is a madman and a fanatical Nazi, and he will do anything for his cause. And when I say anything, I mean anything."

General Meier, attired in his black-leather SS topcoat, sat on a crate of Zyklon B and looked at the other crates of the chemical in the basement of Gestapo headquarters. He was all alone, and it was shortly after one o'clock in the morning. He smoked a cigarette and wondered what to do about the poison gas. Throughout the day, ever since his *Fuehrer* had appointed him commandant of the garrison at Metz, he'd been having doubts about using the gas. He knew it would turn Metz into a sea of corpses and realized that the Americans probably would retaliate. They might even drop poison gas on Berlin. His act might raise the war to an entirely new level of destruction.

But, on the other hand, did the *Fuehrer* himself not say, in a speech before a gathering of SS officers, that if Germany lost the war, it would deserve to be overrun by barbarians, and did he not also say it was good that the German people themselves were feeling the war personally because that would make them more determined and fanatical about winning.

Also, didn't the *Fuehrer* give him permission to do anything he wanted in the defense of Metz? Might not gas warfare win the battle Hitler wanted so much to win, and if the Americans wanted to use gas, too, well so could Germany, in greater quantities than the Americans. Gas warfare, after all, was nothing new. It had been a commonly used weapon during the First World War. At Ypres, the German army turned it loose for the first time, and the British line melted away in front of it. The Germans won a great victory, and might that not happen tomorrow in Metz? With him, General Meier in command?

A victory beyond his wildest imagination?

Electrified by the thought, Meier stood up and paced back and forth amid the crates of Zyklon B. *Yes, I'll do it, I'll do it, I'll do it!* he thought. *Tomorrow I'll have the stuff carried up to the courtyard, and we'll set it off. First thing in the morning.*

Who knows, perhaps it will change the course of this war?

As General Meier paced the floor in the basement of Gestapo headquarters, Mahoney and the five men with him crossed the German lines on the same length of railroad track that Colonel Knoedler had used. They continued moving along the tracks, staying in the shadows and maintaining strict silence.

They all wore black SS uniforms and SS helmets. Their weapons were Schneisser submachine guns, and Colonel Knoedler had told them the password for the night. Meanwhile, XX Corps was subjecting the Germans to a heavy artillery bombardment, hoping to cause confusion and help camouflage the movements of the American commandos.

Capt. Harry Engel, the officer in charge of the group, held up his hand. They stopped, and he looked at his map. Like Mahoney, he spoke German fluently. His parents were Germans who'd emigrated to America a few years before the First World War. He had a big, square German face with a prominent nose and a strong jaw. His voice was deep and strong, and Mahoney thought he was very impressed with himself, for reasons Mahoney could not yet discern.

Also in the group were Sgt. George Beerbower, the child of German-born parents like Engel; Cpl. Raymond Collins, who had studied German culture before the war and had visited Germany many times, and Pfc. Jack Frohlich, born in Germany of Jewish parents who'd emigrated to America in 1931 when it appeared to them that nothing could prevent the Nazis from coming to power.

"I think we should get out of this track now," Engel said, "and start moving into the city."

They climbed the side of the ditch and began walking toward the center of the city as artillery shells exploded around them. Mahoney looked at his watch and hoped they could get everything over with by morning because he didn't want to walk around in broad daylight behind German lines if he could help it.

"Halt!"

They stopped, realizing they had reached the first sentries.

"Who goes there!"

"Captain Engel of Company Two," said Engel, using his real name and rank.

"Advance to be recognized."

Engel and the others moved forward, seeing two sentries aiming rifles at them. One of the sentries asked for the password, and Engel told him the one General Knoedler had given him, hoping it was still operative.

"Pass on," said one of the sentries, and Engel knew it was.

The group passed the sentries, and Mahoney breathed a sigh of relief. He'd been ready to whip around his submachine gun and start firing, but it hadn't been necessary yet.

The five American soldiers made their way into the center of Metz, feeling naked in the midst of so many German soldiers and German tanks, with American shells falling everywhere. Mahoney began to wish that he'd been sent in alone to do this job because he thought one person would attract less attention than five. But in the confusion of battle, as the Germans were preparing to fight last-ditch battles for the defense of Metz, no one noticed them. The artillery barrage from XX Corps kept the Germans too busy.

At 0325 hours, the American soldiers turned on to the Rue Serpenaise and saw Gestapo headquarters straight ahead.

Colonel Knoedler had explained the layout of the building to them, and they knew where to find General Meier's office. The building formerly had been the main headquarters of a wine wholesale business, and the cellars where wine had been aged now were used for incarcerating and torturing real and imagined enemies of the Reich.

"Well, are we ready?" Captain Engel asked.

Nobody said he wasn't, so they lined up and marched toward the front gate of the building. When they reached the gate, Engel ordered them to stop, then he marched to the sentry, who saluted him. The sentry asked for the password, and Engel gave it to him. The sentry opened the gate, and the five Americans marched on to the grounds of Gestapo head- quarters. Another sentry opened the front door, and they entered the building.

Now they no longer could chat among themselves and make plans. All they could do was behave like SS men and try to follow the plan they'd concocted in General Donovan's office, and that plan had been quite simple: to find out where Meier was, kill him, and get away somehow. Mahoney hoped some of the Germans had noticed that no American shells were falling on the building, although they were landing in the vicinity. He hoped none of them might start wondering why.

They walked through the corridors of the building, their hobnailed boots striking hard on the wooden floors. They passed SS men with worried looks on their faces, attired just like them. Finally, they came to the office of General Meier.

"I would like to speak with General Meier at once!" Captain Engel said to the secretary, an SS man.

"I'm afraid he's not in, sir."

"Could you tell me where he is, please?"

"I believe he's in the basement."

"The basement?"

"Yes, in his quarters down there."

"Thank you."

Engel and the others turned around and made their way to the stairs that led to the basement. Mahoney was starting to get a little worried; the longer they roamed the building, the more likely they'd be noticed. Finally, they reached the stairs that led to the basement. They descended them and came to a door made of iron bars.

"Yes?" asked the sergeant behind the door.

"I have an urgent message from the front for General Meier. Is he down here?"

"As a matter of fact he is, captain. Right this way."

The sergeant opened the door, and the five Americans entered the notorious dungeons of the Metz Gestapo headquarters. It reminded Mahoney of the Gestapo dungeon on the Avenue Foch in Paris, which he'd helped to capture along with a few hundred French *maquis*. The sergeant directed them to the rooms where General Meier was.

"He's alone?" asked Engel in an offhand way.

"Yes."

The American soldiers followed the directions the SS sergeant had given them, passing down a series of corridors and hearing screams of pain from all directions. Finally, they came to a quiet part of the dungeon area and saw a sentry standing in front of a door.

"I have an urgent message for General Meier," Captain Engel said.

"I'm sorry, sir," the sentry said, "but he's asleep right now, and he left word that he did not wish to be disturbed."

"I said it's an emergency!" Engel told him.

The sentry was unmoved. "I'm sorry, sir, but I have my orders."

Mahoney silently removed his bayonet from its scabbard and moved to the side of the sentry.

"I'm not leaving here," Engel said, "until I speak with General Meier!"

"Why don't you speak with his adjutant, Colonel Reiter?"

"Because I don't want to speak with his adjutant. I want to speak with General Meier himself!"

"I'm sorry sir but—"

Mahoney lunged, clasped one hand over the sentry's mouth, and plunged his bayonet to the hilt in the sentry's heart. The sentry went limp, and Mahoney let him fall to the floor. Sergeant Beerbower opened the door, and they entered a dark room, Mahoney dragging the dead sentry with him.

"Who's there?" asked the sleepy voice of General Meier. A light went on in a room down the corridor.

"Captain Engel!"

"Who?"

Private, First Class Frohlich closed the door behind them, and they walked down the corridor toward the light.

"I left strict orders that I was not to be disturbed!" General Meier complained. "Who's there?"

The five American soldiers entered the bedroom, Mahoney holding his bloodied knife behind his back.

"What's the meaning of this!" demanded General Meier in his blue pajamas. "Who are you!"

General Meier reached underneath his pillow for his pistol, and the Americans opened fire on him. They'd wanted to kill him silently, but it was too late for that now. Their bullets ripped into General Meier and splattered his blood all over the white sheets of his bed. He writhed and twisted, clawing at the holes in his body, but then his heart stopped beating, and he was still.

Corporal Collins stepped forward and took his pulse. "He's dead," he said.

"Let's get out of here," Mahoney said, putting the bayonet away.

They looked at each other anxiously, knowing that it wouldn't be easy to get out of that basement. They also knew that the longer they waited, the worse it would be for them.

Captain Engel led them out of the room and down the corridor. They opened the door to the hallway, looked around, and left General Meier's quarters, running toward the stairs.

Three SS men rounded the corner in front of them. "Halt!" one of them shouted.

The American soldiers opened fire on them and kept running. The Germans returned their fire, and their bullets cut down Corporal Collins before they themselves were shot to bits. The four remaining Americans jumped over their bodies and continued their wild dash toward the stairs. They turned a corner and saw a dozen Germans running toward them. Mahoney and the others backed up, spraying them with bullets, shooting down some of the Germans, but one of the

German bullets passed through Captain Engel's head, and he fell at Mahoney's feet.

"This way!" Mahoney said.

He stepped over Engel's body and ran back toward Meier's room, with Beerbower and Frohlich behind him.

"Halt!" shouted the Germans behind them.

The Germans fired, and their bullets richocheted around the corridor, but the three Americans disappeared around a corner and ran swiftly into General Meier's room, bolting the lock behind them.

"What do we do now?" asked Frohlich, who was round-shouldered and had eyes that turned down at the corners.

"There must be another exit down here," Mahoney replied.

They ran through the suite of rooms, opening doors frantically. They found closets full of clothes and food, more rooms, and a small kitchen. Then Mahoney pushed open a door and found another corridor.

"Let's go!" he said.

They ran down the corridor and came to a flight of stairs. Vaulting up the stairs, they reached a door that was locked. Mahoney lowered his submachine gun, fired at the lock, and blew it away. He crashed through the door and landed in an office area where two SS clerks sat at a desk. They stood and looked at the three Americans in alarm. The Americans riddled their bodies with bullets and filled the room with gunsmoke.

Beerbower opened the door to the corridor and saw hordes of SS men running toward him from all directions. He pulled back the door and closed it, turning to Mahoney.

"The corridor is full of krauts!" he said.

Mahoney spun around and saw a window. He picked up a chair, threw it through the window, and cried: "Follow me!"

Running across the room, he jumped out the window, holding his arms and his carbine in front of his face. A piece of jagged glass slashed across the side of his ribs, and he dropped to the grass lawn. Germans were shouting everywhere. Frohlich and Beerbower fell to the lawn and rolled over. Mahoney pulled a hand grenade out of his pocket and ran toward the steel fence that surrounded the building. He hurled the grenade at the gate and dropped to his stomach; the explosion blew a hole in the metal bars.

"Let's go!" Mahoney said.

They ran through the opening as Germans fired at them from the windows of the building. Other Germans fired from the lawn, and one of the bullets brought down Sergeant Beerbower.

Frohlich bent over Beerbower. "He's still alive!"

Just then, a bullet hit Frohlich in the chest, and he fell on top of Beerbower. Mahoney, meanwhile, kept running because he knew it would be instant death to stop for any reason. He ran in a zigzag pattern, heading straight for the battered buildings across the street. He knew that once he got in that mess, he'd have a chance of getting away, but it looked as far away as China.

Bullets whistled past his ears and kicked up fragments of cobblestone around his feet. Blood dripped out of the cut in his side, and he expected a bullet in his back at any moment. He took a running dive and landed behind a pile of rubble on the other side of the street. Protected for a moment, he took a few deep breaths.

"After him!" shouted a German.

Keeping his head low, Mahoney crept into a nearby alley and at its other end ran like mad across the next street. He was moving into the area where American artillery shells were falling, and he continued to run around ruined buildings and through the hallways of buildings that were still standing, continually changing his direction and not stopping for anything, not even to look at the wound in his side. Artillery shells exploded near him, and he kept going. German soldiers told him to halt, but he paid no attention to them. He ran with all his strength and finally reached a desolate part of the city that looked as if it might have been the poor section before the bombs started falling.

Mahoney hid in some shadows, trying to catch his breath and looked at the old, broken-down buildings. Germans liked to set up command post and billets in fancy chateaus and mansions, so he didn't think any would come near this neighborhood unless they were forced to fight here. He decided it might be a good idea to go into one of the cellars and hide until the Americans took the rest of the city. Then he could come out and not have to go through the danger of trying to pass through the German lines. Presumably, an alert had been posted for renegade SS men. This definitely would be a good time to drop out of sight.

Silently, like an alley cat, Mahoney crept toward the nearest building, holding his hand to his bleeding side. *I really can't take much more of this war,* he thought. *What I need now is about two years of R&R.*

TWENTY-FIVE

On November 23, General Patton rode into Metz in the turret of a tank. It had stopped raining, and the sun was shining. All resistance had ceased in the city the previous afternoon. Behind the tank was a column of other tanks, jeeps, and trucks.

Patton was ebullient as he gazed at the buildings of the battered city. Metz hadn't been captured by assault since A.D. 451, but his Third Army had taken the old fortress city in only fourteen days. Surely, the world would remember the Third Army and him for that.

Soldiers along the road stopped whatever they were doing and saluted Patton, who saluted them back. *What a great thing victory is,* Patton thought. *It raises morale more than anything else and makes the men confident.* Some of the men cheered after they saluted, and Patton gave them thumbs up.

The convoy rolled toward the center of the city and stopped before an old municipal building that was the new headquarters for XX Corps. Patton climbed down from the tank and, surrounded by staff officers and aides, marched toward the building. The MPs guarding the building saluted smartly, and General Walker, the commander of the XX Corps, came down the front steps to meet him, followed by an entourage of his own that included his division commanders, among them General Donovan of the Hammerhead Division.

Patton shook hands with Walker and congratulated him for a job well done. "I knew you could do it, Bobby," he said, "and I knew the weather wouldn't stop you."

"Well, it was touch and go for a while there," Walker said with a grin. "That poison gas had us worried for a while there."

"Yes," agreed Patton, "and I want to give medals to the men who took care of that."

"Only one of them came back," said Walker as the group of officers entered the building.

"Only one?" asked Patton. "Who was he?"

"A master sergeant named Mahoney. He's in the Hammerhead Division, sir."

Patton touched his hand to his cheek and looked at the ceiling. "Mahoney. It seems to me I've heard that name before."

"He's practically a legend in the Hammerhead Division, sir. Used to be in the Rangers. Speaks German and French fluently."

"Is that so?" asked Patton.

"He's also the heavyweight champion of the Hammerhead Division."

"Hmmmm."

They entered the conference room, and Patton appeared deep in thought. The officers gathered around the map table, waiting for him to speak. Patton leaned on the edge of the table, his eyebrows knitted together.

"You know," he said to General Walker, "we've been having a lot of trouble behind our lines with German commando teams who've been blowing up ammo dumps and communication lines, ambushing troops, and stuff like that. We haven't had much luck at catching them, but I just was thinking that maybe we should sick this Mahoney character after them. If he's as sharp as you say he is, maybe he can track them down. What do you think?"

Walker shrugged. "It's as good an idea as any I've heard. We can give him as many men as he thinks he needs and turn him loose. He's just liable to catch the bastards."

"Good," said Patton. "Take care of it and keep me posted." He looked down at the map and pulled off his leather gloves. "Okay, gentlemen, now we've got Metz. Let's try to figure out where we're going next."

"The most important horror collection of the year."

—*Locus*

DARK FORCES

Edited by Kirby McCauley

(14801-x) $3.50

**Including a complete new short novel
by Stephen King**

This new volume of 23 chillers contains new works by a star-studded roster of authors. You'll find spine-tingling tales from Davis Grubb, Ray Bradbury, Edward Gorey, Robert Aickman, Joe Haldeman, Dennis Etchison, Karl Edward Wagner, Lisa Tuttle, Ramsey Campbell, T.E.D. Klein, and many other masters of horror.

Get ready for terror as you encounter slug-like creatures who inhabit New York City's sewers, zombies who become all-night store clerks in California, a young boy who is kidnapped in his very own bed, and a multitude of horrifying beings and events.

Available in September wherever paperbacks are sold or directly from Bantam Books. Include $1.00 for postage and handling and send check to Bantam Books, Dept. DF, 414 East Golf Road, Des Plaines, Illinois 60016. Allow 4–6 weeks for delivery.

The most explosive book on organized crime since
The Valachi Papers

THE LAST MAFIOSO
by Ovid Demaris

Over 3 months on
The New York Times
Bestseller List!

Jimmy "The Weasel" Fratianno was the mob's top killer—until he became the government's most cooperative witness. Now the highest ranking mafioso ever to "turn" takes you deep into the underworld in this sizzling expose that stunned the Mafia's Big Boys and has made headlines all across the country.

- What *really* happened to Jimmy Hoffa?
- What was the real CIA-Mafia plot to kill Castro?
- Why did a mobster share his mistress with a U.S. president?
- Has La Cosa Nostra tainted the Reagan cabinet?

The answers are all in *THE LAST MAFIOSO*—the sensational national bestseller that reveals the mob's most shocking family secrets.

Read THE LAST MAFIOSO, on sale October 15, 1981 wherever Bantam paperbacks are sold.